Whirlpool

And Other Short Stories

Whirlpool
And Other Short Stories

JOHN DURHAM

THE CHOIR PRESS

First published in the United Kingdom in 2019 by
The Choir Press

ISBN 978-1-78963-075-6

Contents

———◦◉◦———

Acknowledgements

Firstly, to my family and close friends for their unwavering support and encouragement. To Margaret, for putting up with my endless story ideas. To Luke, for his help on the first story, 'Whirlpool'.

Again, to Meg Humphries and Choir Press for their professionalism, support and encouragement.

Whirlpool

Nicholas, or Nic as he liked to be called, had just completed his second year at Nottingham Trent University, doing Environmental Studies. He was now in the passenger seat of a rickety old van driven, by Bob, along some long, winding country road in south Shropshire. He had volunteered his summer months to help out at the Shropshire Wildlife Trust. Bob, who was driving, was in his mid to late fifties, stocky build approximately five foot six inches tall with a balding head of greying hair and spectacles that hung dangerously off the end of his nose.

'Right, if I drop you off here at this bridge,' he said, pointing at his sat nav, 'I'll then pick you up here, at this bridge in say, two hours. That should give you enough time.'

The River Rea, also called the 'Neen', was Nic's office for the afternoon. This small river flows on into the 'Neme' and then eventually into the mighty Severn.

'That sounds fine,' said Nic. 'If I'm going to be a bit late, I'll message you.'

'Brill,' replied Bob, not taking his eyes off the road.

Nic's third-year thesis was to be on the decline of British birds that rely on water for a habitat. Not an exciting subject to most people, but a worrying one all the same.

His mission this lovely afternoon was to spot and record any kingfishers on this four-mile stretch of water. Normally you'd get the farmer's permission to wander on his land, but with so many farms bordering the small river, logistically it proved impossible to contact and get approval from all concerned, so Nic, with high green waders tied securely around his waist, had to walk up the middle of the river, therefore not needing anyone's permission, only Severn Trent Water, who were very happy to approve his request.

The Severn is one of the major rivers in the United Kingdom. Starting from its humblest source way up in the Welsh moorland hills, it reaches the sea at the Severn Estuary, arguably one of the highest tidal reaches in the world.

On its meandering way down the borderlands between England and Wales, it provides both power and irrigation to farms and communities in its path. Not forgetting the tourism it brings in with rowing clubs, kayaking and fishing all along its length.

Bob's erratic braking brought Nic to his senses; he realised quickly that they were approaching the bridge where he was to start his project.

The van stopped, Nic looked at Bob, who gave him the 'thumbs-up' sign. Nic jumped out, patted the side of the van and leant against the side of the bridge.

The van drove off, spluttering and backfiring into the distance; a wave out the driver's side window from Bob, and he was standing there alone in the silence of a summer afternoon. Nic checked his equipment: a GPS system (needed if he came across anything important), a log book and waterproof pen to record anything unusual.

He made his way past the end of the bridge and down into the river. Upstream was his planned route. It was a lovely July afternoon, hot and humid, and the sunlight sparkled off the eddying water as it flowed downstream. It was afternoons like this that proved to Nic that he had chosen his career path well. He just hoped there were plenty of jobs out there when he qualified and that he wasn't stuck in an office job somewhere or a call centre ... or even worse, a burger outfit!

A small splash ahead of him brought him quickly to his senses. He didn't see what it was so was cross with himself for his daydreaming. He promised himself he'd be extra alert from now on.

An hour into his journey upriver and Nic was almost halfway, nothing spectacular to report, though plenty of birdsong and birds to spot – he had already recorded blackbirds, thrushes, wrens, robins and plenty of willow warblers and chaffinches. A flitting family of long-tailed tits feeding through the over-hanging willow, busy chatting to each other, but no kingfishers to report.

Nic had only seen one kingfisher in his life: a flash of brilliant blue caught out of the corner of his eye when he was seventeen, sat on the banks of the Severn just south of Shrewsbury with his then girlfriend Kate. Kate didn't see anything and Nic was sure if he'd been on his own he would have followed it to see this magnificent bird in the flesh, so to speak. But his love for Kate had no bounds at that time in his life, so they sat there holding hands and chatting about their future. Kate was brilliant at maths so was looking at a career in astronomy or something similar. Her dad was a lecturer in physics at the Open University and six months after they had sat lovingly together on that riverbank she was off to America, where her dad had got a new job. She had messaged him a few times to say she had attained a post at Cornell University somewhere near New York, a million miles from the sleepy suburbs of Shrewsbury.

Nic had written back but by then Kate had taken second place to his A levels, so sadly they had drifted apart. Nic wondered how she was doing and hoped she was enjoying her chosen path as much as he was.

He stumbled on something in the water, and again chastised himself for daydreaming. He looked down and, after removing his size-ten boot out of the hole he'd stumbled into, he stood there mesmerised, watching a small whirlpool form where his boot had been. Like watching water flowing down the plug-hole in the bath, water was disappearing into this hole (for want of a better word) at a surprisingly fast rate. Nic got out his GPS and recorded the exact spot.

He checked his watch – he'd wasted too much time and Bob would be waiting for him. He didn't want an angry Bob driving back to Shrewsbury so he left the small whirlpool behind and made his way on up river to his meeting place, the next bridge.

Bob and the van were waiting for him. It was five minutes past their scheduled meet time but Bob was okay with that as he'd been able to sneak a quick fag while he was waiting. He couldn't smoke in the van; company policy.

'Spot any?' were Bob's first words as he climbed the bank by the side of the bridge. It was a bit slippy and Nic made heavy weather of it in his waist high waders

4

… But expecting a helping-hand from Bob? No way.

Bob's philosophy was 'Bob First'.

Nic scrambled round the parapet of the bridge, slightly out of breath. 'No, none today.'

'Never mind, you've a few more rivers to explore yet this summer. Hop in, or I'll be late back for my tea, and Mrs Bob doesn't like Bob to be late!' This amused Nic and a wry smile floated across his lips as the van choked into life.

Bob dropped Nic off at 193 Abbey Foregate, where Nic's bike was stored. He then had a ten-minute cycle ride to his parents' house.

'Did you feel it?!' came a shout from the kitchen as he opened the back door.

'Feel what, Mum?'

'The earthquake!'

'What?!'

'There was an earthquake this afternoon, just south of Bridgnorth. Not very big – 3.1 on the Richter, they said on the news. Typical strength for Britain, though.'

'Wow, Mum. No, I didn't feel it, I was inches deep in water most of the afternoon with waist-high waders on. I wouldn't have felt Krakatoa!'

'Kraka-who?'

'Never mind.'

Nic's mum had never worked. He supposed she would be called a 'stay-at-home mum' these days but Nic was grateful that she was there every day after school, giving him encouragement in anything he'd tried and failed at.

She was devastated when Nic left home, as most mums are when their child goes off to university or starts working away. She had never shown this openly to Nic but he had an inkling of how she'd felt. Having Nic home for the whole of the summer was heaven to Maria. She never showed it but Nic felt it every day he arrived back from work.

Nic's dad had passed a year earlier: prostate cancer, the silent killer for the male population. Nic had just gone off to university when his mum had rung him with the devastating news. His dad, Mike, had been given less than six months but had survived ten. Thankfully, Nic had completed his first year by then and was there to support his mum at the end.

'I should have felt it, Mum. I was very near the epicentre, so it seems,' he murmured as he studied the map provided by the news station.

Ummm, thought Nic, the small whirlpool, maybe there is a connection. He couldn't be sure but in future he thought he'd keep a careful watch on anything unusual happening in south Shropshire over the next few weeks.

He'd read somewhere that animal behaviour and water movement are very good indicators of earthquakes and possibly of more to come.

The next morning Bob was there at Abbey Foregate biting at the bit to get going as Nic cycled into the yard at the back and parked up his bike.

Just a little tap with his finger on his wristwatch was enough for Nic to jump in without any fuss.

'It's the Neme today, is it?' said Bob.

'Yes, a bit further on today, I'm afraid,' said Nic, hoping his apology would go down well with sulky Bob. They travelled in silence for most of the way, just the usual curt expletives from Bob about other drivers on the road.

They reached their starting point a little bit earlier than planned, and Nic didn't want to lose any more time, so he was out of the van in record time and ready with his equipment for Bob to drive off. No courteous wave from Bob this morning. Nic shrugged his shoulders and made his way down into the river.

His first thought was that the river level seemed to be a bit low, lower than he was expecting, and it didn't take him long to find out why. Just around the next bend in the river, he heard it before he saw it, the similar sound of water running down a plughole. A whirlpool bigger than the one yesterday, as wide as the river at this point. He wondered how big the hole was. He wasn't going to put his size-ten foot anywhere near this one.

This has got to have something to do with the earthquake yesterday, surely, thought Nic, but where was all the water going, and what was happening further downstream? He clambered out onto the bank and past the swirling babble, recording the exact spot with his GPS as he did so. Wading back in, he then carried on with his work upstream.

With his mind on other things, he almost missed it – a kingfisher sat on top of a fence post barely fifty feet in front of him. Bright brilliant blue and even more so in the sunlight.

Nic stood statue-still for minutes, it seemed like. The post the bird was sat on was obviously one of its favourite perches, the post leaning slightly out over a bend in the river with a slow-flowing, almost stagnant pool below. Suddenly a flash of blue, a splash, another flash of blue and it was gone. Nic walked up to the spot and recorded it on his GPS. A wave of emotion came over him – finally, a kingfisher! The smile on his face lasted for the rest of the afternoon.

Bob was waiting for him at their reunion point, a slight smile on his face. Nic took a quick look at his watch – five minutes early, hopefully the journey back would be a bit less fraught than the ride down that morning. Nic thought of Mrs Bob getting the tea ready and the smile got broader on his face.

'You look pleased with yourself,' came the voice of Bob, who was leaning over the bridge.

'Yes, finally recorded one.'

'Good stuff. Come on, we can't dawdle.'

The journey back was a lot less fraught. Nic plucked up the courage to mention the two whirlpools he'd discovered and the fact of the recent earthquake in the vicinity. Bob listened intently, which was reassuring to Nic as he'd expected any mention of his thoughts would be pushed to one side without any recognition.

'I think you should mention this ... upstairs' – Nic used the word he'd heard Bob use for the hierarchy of the organisation. 'Perhaps we should give tomorrow's river trip a miss. I'll mention this upstairs in the morning.'

'Good stuff,' said Bob. 'Well done for keeping your eyes open.' Wow, a plaudit from Bob! Could the afternoon get any better?

The smell as he entered the kitchen told Nic it could possibly be, yes, Mum's home-made lasagne, Nic's favourite.

His cycle ride the next morning was very thoughtful; hopefully his bosses would see the connection and put some resources in place. His early-morning meeting with the secretary and CEO of the organisation went very well. They both took on board the connection with the recent earthquake and the water loss as his GPS locations showed that both whirlpools were relative to the epicentre of the quake. The CEO suggested that all available manpower should go out and check all the river tributaries to the Severn in a thirty-mile radius of the epicentre of the earthquake.

Nic was amazed the next day on entering the office at Abbey Foregate. Everyone was on high alert and every available warden and volunteer was actually out there looking for whirlpools.

They had targeted all the rivers in Shropshire and North Herefordshire closest to the epicentre. Nic's initial thoughts were 'What have I done?'

Resources in any of the country's Wildlife Trusts were stretched any day of the week so to put a large proportion of their personnel into action meant serious business. Nic's worries were well founded as more and more reports came in, recording whirlpools in all the major tributaries leading into the River Severn, virtually on a line from Bridgnorth to Hereford. This was a major worry as all of these tributaries fed the River Severn, so thoughts of effective drainage, irrigation and tourism obviously worried the hierarchy of the trust, whom felt responsible for those downstream.

Half past four in the afternoon and the CEO stood up and said, 'Right, what do we do now?' No one came up with a positive response except Nic. He couldn't believe he'd stood up, but here he was, face-to-face with the CEO.

'I, um, I think there's worse to come,' said Nic.

'Explain yourself!'

'Well,' said Nic, 'I've looked at recent earthquakes in Italy, and Sichuan in China. Both reported unusual movements in water tables.'

A movement to his left and Bob stood up.

'I don't know if anyone here remembers the Haicheng earthquake in 1975. Groundwater movements and animal behaviour had a great deal to do with the authorities being able to warn everyone of an impending earthquake. Thousands of lives were saved, the one and only time an earthquake had been accurately predicted. Let's take their knowledge and Nic's observations and warn everyone in the area another earthquake is very probable and almost imminent.'

'That's a big call!' said the CEO.

'Can we afford not to?' said Bob.

A show of hands all around the room made it obvious to the CEO that a call to a local or even national news station was required.

On the cycle ride home Nic couldn't get his head around Bob's support for his theory. There was more to Bob than Nic could easily explain.

'Mum, you've got to put the TV news on tonight!' were Nic's first words as he walked into the kitchen.

'Yes, fine, dear. You seem very excited about something. Is everything okay in work?'

'Too much to explain at the moment, Mum, but yes, work is fine. Living up to all expectations, and more.'

Maria had made another of Nic's favourites, spaghetti bolognese. They sat together on the sofa in the lounge, meals on their laps, waiting for the main news bulletin to come on.

There, outside Abbey Foregate, the leader of the local authority and the CEO of Shropshire Wildlife Trust both stood in front of the country's media to announce that it was likely there would be a major earthquake in the area, and all authorities, local and national, should take immediate steps to protect human life and infrastructure.

'Oh my God!' said Mum. 'Are we going to be alright?'

You'll be fine,' said Nic. 'Nothing's going to stop you making lasagne!'

A slap on the arm told Nic this wasn't the time for a flippant remark.

'Sorry, Mum. Yes, we'll be fine. Now the warning has gone out, everyone will be vigilant, so early warnings of any impending danger will be acted upon.'

'What will happen to your kingfishers? Don't they need lots of water to fish?'

'The kingfishers' breeding season is over, so hopefully the young will have all fledged by now, so they will move further away to find good fishing pools and take their youngsters with them. This problem isn't country-wide, Mum. It's located within thirty miles of the epicentre of the earthquake. Wildlife is very resilient and much more adaptable to environment changes than us humans – that might be our downfall in the end.'

'Oh, don't say that!'

'That will be when we are long gone, Mum.'

Nic had a sleepless night. Had he opened a Pandora's box? Only the next few days or weeks would tell.

Deadwood

---◦⊚⊚◦---

Chin Hoy was of Chinese descendancy, but three generations of the family had lived in Malaysia now, ever since his grandfather had fled the civil war in China in 1930. Chin was a biotechnologist and worked at a government establishment a few miles south of the capital, Kuala Lumpur.

His pet project, and one he had kept secret from his employers for most of his time there, was to create, by artificial engineering, a plant that could devour other plants of a certain DNA. Chin's thinking was to create a plant that could get rid of invasive plants from other countries which were causing problems for mainly agriculture and water management.

He was thinking of Japanese knotweed, Himalayan balsam and even the beautiful rhododendron. He had been working on 'his project' for just over twelve years and for the past two years had been working on one particular plant that was showing much promise. One thing worrying Chin now was that he had gone out to tend to his plant this particular morning and found that it had grown this tall yellow trumpet-like flower out of its centre core, standing on a strong purple stalk about two and a half metres high. He worried that this would be spotted by his bosses as the original plant was a low-growing large green-leafed plant.

Next morning after arriving for work he was straight down to check out the plant and was surprised to find the tall trumpet-like flower now lying on the ground, withered. 'What's happened here?' he thought to himself – then a worrying scenario occurred to him: this plant might have seeded overnight. He really hoped it hadn't.

The spot he'd chosen for his experiment was a far-flung corner of the establishment, well out of sight of the main building block, next to a deer park, where all manner of native and foreign deer roamed at will. Between the government establishment and deer park ran an eight-foot-high galvanised steel chain-link fence, high enough to stop the deer leaping over but worryingly open enough for a seed to fall through, he now realised. He checked the remains of the trumpet flower, and his worse fears were evident: this flower had definitely seeded itself – but was it one seed or many? Chin could only surmise and worry on what he might have done.

*

Carrie Long was horticulture manager for a large country estate just north of Oxford, England. Carrie had a first-class honours degree in horticulture from Nottingham Trent University and during her final year had even been invited to Highgrove to view and record the wide variety of flora there.

Her final thesis was entitled 'Will Our Native Flora Survive the Relentless Progression of Engineered Crops?'

Carrie's daily job was to visit as much of the estate as she could and to list and report all future works that required attention, like new planting, hedge cutting or tree felling, all within the confines of good management and the need for sustainability.

The estate had a large herd of roe deer, of which it was proud. A similar post to Carrie's was held by John Davis, the 'Herd Manager'. He had the job of managing the herd all year round which included the strength of the stock, ensuring a good supply of both stags and mature hinds. The main part of his job was controlling the size of the herd every autumn by natural wastage, selling good stock on to other estates or by culling, which he tried to keep to a minimum. Culling was the thing Carrie hated the most, and she was always on John's back in late autumn to minimise the death toll.

It was a mid-summer's morning and Carrie had pulled up in her open Land Rover next to a small copse of hawthorn at the edge of Five-acre Wood. Carrie decided the copse had to be removed to let more light and air into that side of the wood, so she recorded what was there, the size and how much should be removed. While studying the internals of the copse, though, she noticed a plant she didn't recognise. This annoyed her intensely as she prided herself on knowing all of the flora native to the British Isles.

This sample had large dark green leaves lying close to the ground with a purple stalk growing out of its centre, about half a metre high. She recorded everything on her iPad and left, after creating a plan for the removal of the copse for the ground staff to follow the following week. She continued on her drive around the estate, on the lookout for anything that needed attention, but her mind kept slipping back to that damn plant. What was it, and what was it doing there?

It was Friday afternoon and she had finished her drive around the eastern part of the estate and her thoughts suddenly turned to a boozy night at the local pub and the quiz league. She was the only female member of the four-strong team and it was obvious to everyone it was her knowledge of all plants native and beyond that had got her onto the team – that and she also loved the company and banter every Friday night.

*

Monday morning and Mike Jarman, head grounds-keeper, checked out the jobs and tasks for the week ahead. He read Carrie's report on the hawthorn copse and thought that this would be an easy job for the boys to start that afternoon. He respected Carrie's position and diligently reported to her every week, although he was twelve years her senior.

Carrie was out on the north boundary of the estate checking out the laurel hedge they had planted two years earlier. She was there to make sure the deer hadn't stripped out the young shoots, thus rendering them useless as a tall hedge plant. She took the call from Mike and listened intently.

'That's not possible,' said Carrie. 'Last Friday after-noon there was only one plant there! An unusual one, I'll admit, but now this! Give me ten minutes and I'll be right with you.'

The phone call Carrie had received from Mike was one of amazement and wonder: the hawthorn copse she had recorded had gone, and in its place was a group of low-lying large green-leafed plants that no one could recognise. The leaves were half a metre across and about twenty plants had now covered the area where the copse had once been. The main plant at the centre of what was the copse had obviously flowered but the flowering stalk had now collapsed on the ground, half-withered. The remains of the hawthorn copse was evidently there but all the trunks and branches were lying on the surrounding area, paper-thin and dry. It looked to Mike as if the life had been sucked out of them.

When Carrie arrived, Mike and his boys were busy setting up a barrier around the area. 'That's a good idea,' said Carrie. 'Keep the deer well away until we find out what this thing is?' Don't want them feeding on it until we discover its heritage!'

'We'll be done before we knock off this evening.'

'Great, Mike. Thanks.'

John had been out all afternoon checking the herds around the 300-acre park. At that moment he pulled up on his quad bike.

'What's happened here?'

'We're not sure yet,' said Carrie. 'Got some invasive plant, by the look of it.'

'Good idea to keep the deer away. Is it poisonous?'

'No idea, I need to take a sample to find out.'

A herd of roe deer not far away were very interested in what the group of people were doing and watched them intently.

'That's a fine-looking stag fronting that herd of roe over there,' Carrie observed.

'Yes' said John. 'He arrived last week from Malaysia. Taken to his job very well, wouldn't you say?'

'Very impressive he looks too, but why Malaysia?'

'We needed new stock, so we sourced a herd, in fact the descendants of the original herd here. Some were taken out there as a gift by the then 4th Earl in 1835.'

'He looks very interested in what we're doing,' said Carrie.

'Well, this copse here had been his favourite place to sleep since he arrived. Don't know where he'll go next?' questioned Mike.

'I think we need to clear this, dig it all out and dispose of it – by fire, preferably,' said Carrie.

'I'm with you on that. Don't like the look of this plant at all!'

'Any ideas on why it's here or where it's come from?' said Mike.

'No, nothing yet. I'll need a sample of a leaf though, maybe check it out at Kew. I know the assistant head gardener there.'

'I'll log the clearance job into the works time sheet, should get it done before the end of the week.'

*

Jeremy Walsh had been at Kew for fifteen years, having originally joined as a junior landscaper at twenty-three years old and toiled hard, working his way up to a top position.

'Hi Carrie, got your email last night. What can I help you with?'

'Hi Jeremy, thanks so much for seeing me. I've got a plant on the estate I don't recognise so I have brought a sample over for you to identify, if you can?'

'Something YOU can't identify, Carrie? That IS interesting!'

'Thanks, but it's annoying me. I would love your input.'

'No problems. Let's see what you've got.'

Carrie put on a pair of plastic gloves and pulled out the whole leaf from a plastic bag she was carrying.

'Wow, that's some specimen, dark green, deep veined and serrated edges,' Jeremy said. 'Where did it come from?'

Carrie explained about the hazel copse and its demise, but also the purple stalk, which she had photographed on her iPad and so held up for him to see.

'That *is* unusual,' said Jeremy. 'Anything else you can tell me about it?'

'Well,' said Carrie, 'something unusual that the head herdsman told me was the new roe deer stag had recently been imported from Malaysia. The hazel copse was his favourite place to sleep.'

'Mmmm, what's the chance he's brought something over with him?'

'That's a possibility,' said Carrie, 'but what?'

'Give me a couple of days and I'll get back to you.'

'Thanks, Jeremy. By the way, it's all looking fantastic here.' She gestured around her at the majestic and richly planted Kew Gardens.

'Cheers, Carrie. Hard work but well worth it for the plaudits.'

Two days later and Jeremy had read something in the Royal Horticultural Society magazine, a small article about a genetic experiment that had gone wrong. A minor geneticist in Malaysia had been carrying out a genetic experiment on his own without government funding or government knowledge. The frantic worry was a seed, or seeds, might have exited the boundary fence, so a search was on for new growth.

Jeremy messaged Carrie the next day: *Checked out a few things, apparently a new invasive plant has been established in Malaysia without government funding or knowledge. The fear is that a seed or seeds had transversed the confines of the establishment and probably got picked up or transported elsewhere. Thinking about your new roe stag!!*

Carrie messaged back: *'Thanks, Jeremy, that's interesting. I'll relay what you've found out to John the herd manager, see what he thinks.*

Carrie found John and his staff erecting some temporary fencing to corral the deer herd into as the new season's bucks and does had to be ear-tagged and at the same time checked over by the local vet.

'Hi Carrie.'

'Hi John, just wondering, what are your thoughts on the new stag?'

'Well, he's certainly taken to his job with a gusto. We brought him over to service the female herd and he's certainly done that already.'

'Anything you can think of that's unusual about him?' asked Carrie.

'No, not really. He likes to be on his own at night though, sleeps away from the main herd, that's all.'

'Do you know exactly where he came from in Malaysia?'

'Somewhere south of the capital, I believe. We've got movement records which will tell us exactly. I'll check it out later and get back to you.'

Carrie decided to keep the information she'd

received from Jeremy secret for a while and to let John get back to her about where this stag actually came from first. She looked once more at this majestic stag and thought on what Jeremy had said. 'What have you brought over with you? I hope it's not going to cause us too much trouble,' she thought.

Carrie was at home that evening making her favourite meal, tuna pasta bake, easy and quick to make and she always added fresh herbs from her own garden. Her phone suddenly rang. Cursing under her breath, wiping her hands, she picked up her mobile.

'Oh, hi, John. What have you found out?'

'Quite a bit actually. The stag came from a herd located on a municipal park just south of the capital, owned and managed by the Malaysian government, right next door to an experimental establishment, also government-run. Seems like they have got a problem – from what I understand, some seeds or seed from an experimental plant might have fallen through the boundary fence. Are you thinking what I'm thinking, or are you way ahead?'

'I might be just ahead of you; my friend at Kew will carry out some tests on the leaf I gave him. We'll see what he comes up with.'

'Did he manage to shed any light on what we've got here?'

'No, he wouldn't commit himself. Let's see what he comes back with. John – perhaps as a precaution if there are any other seeds lying around, and I'm assuming they may have passed through the stag's digestive system, we should be out there collecting all the deer poo we can find in the general area of where the copse stood.'

'I'll get Mike and his lads onto it first thing in the morning.'

Back to completing her pasta bake, Carrie's mind wandered back to the afternoon when she first saw the rogue plant and the purple stalk at its centre. That stalk grew quite high and flowered over the weekend. Why had the flower withered so quickly? It had a strong, defiant stalk when she saw it, but three days later it had collapsed down to nothing. She poured herself a large glass of Sauvignon Blanc and settled down to enjoy her meal. 'Oh dear,' she thought to herself, 'has the damn plant seeded? Maybe that's why the flower faded; it had done its job.'

She completed her meal then picked up her phone to ring John for his thoughts.

John answered straight away; a call from Carrie at nine o' clock in the evening – something must be up.

'Hi Carrie, what's up?'

'Just thinking about our earlier conversation, what if the plant in the copse had seeded over last weekend, we might not just be picking up the prominent stag's poo – we might have to do the whole damn estate!'

'Oh, don't say that, that's an impossible scenario.'

'I'll check the flower out in the morning, see if it has seeded or not.'

'Okay, let's sleep on it!'

'I don't know if I will be able to tonight now,' said Carrie.

*

Next morning, Carrie met John and Mike at the site of the copse. She examined the withered flower head with gloved hands.

21

'Yes, definitely seeded, but how come so quickly, and what or who was the pollinator?'

'Perhaps it's capable of autogamy – self-fertilisation?' said Mike.

'That's entirely possible,' answered Carrie, 'and I'm sure the person or persons who genetically created this monster knew exactly what they were doing!'

'From the reports I've read on the internet, it was one rogue employee,' said John.

'Do we have a name? Can we contact him?' questioned Carrie.

'We need to speak to him if at all possible. It might help us control this here and now. If not, and this gets out into the wider countryside, then it might never be stopped.'

'I'll see if I can find out more,' said John.

Carrie's phone rang – it was Jeremy from Kew, so she put him on speaker.

'Nice timing, Jeremy – we're all here, waiting to find out what you've discovered.'

'Well, I hope you're all ready for this, it's a genetically modified type of Dock Weed, Latin name Rumex Obtusifolius, engineered over years of adaption to actually replace other species, which is what must have happened in your copse. Once adapted, it will quickly duplicate, and take the place of the home species, again which you found in your copse. It will only produce one seed at a time, which is encouraging, but the seed is highly aromatic and therefore attractive to herbivores such as deer, antelope et cetera, who are closely related to sheep, goats and cattle. So, you can see the scenario – if this gets outside the estate it could invade the whole country in a very short time!'

'What sort of timescale are we looking at?'

'I would say years rather than decades.'

'My God, the life of our country's flora and fauna could well be in our hands at this very point in time.'

'I would say you were spot-on with that assumption, Carrie.'

Mike and his team dug up the plants that had invaded the copse in a controlled way and disposed of them. The deer droppings over a wide area around the copse were also collected and disposed of.

*

'Hi John,' said Carrie as she pulled up in her Land Rover next to his a week or so later. 'Still admiring your Malaysian stag, I see?'

'He's a beaut, isn't he?' John replied. 'Hopefully next spring we'll see his beautiful offspring prancing all around here. What are your thoughts now, on that invasive plant you discovered?'

'I'm hoping we've seen the last of it,' said Carrie. 'I got a message from Jeremy this morning. He's heard the Malaysian government believe they have stopped the spread, no new cases have been discovered for over two weeks now.'

'Do you think we've achieved the same here?'

'I really don't know, John. Only time will tell, I suppose. I'm keeping everything crossed for the next month, at least.'

As Carrie drove off, John shouted, 'How's Five-acre Wood doing?'

'Really good now there's plenty of light and air getting in. I knew it was a good idea to remove that copse!!' Carrie drove off with a big smile and a wave.

GravitNess

———⁖⊙⊙⊙⁖———

Cameron Iwan stood on the northern shore of Lake Windermere in Cumbria and looked out across the shimmering clear water.

'Now, I wonder what secrets you hold for me,' he thought to himself.

Cameron stood 5 feet 11 inches tall and had a shock of Celtic auburn hair, greying now around the temples, and a full beard to match.

Cameron had been born and brought up on a small croft in the Outer Hebrides. The croft had been passed down from his grandfather, his father had run it well too, but after his father's death five years earlier Cameron had moved back to keep the family tradition going, only to find out a year later that the local laird had died and his family had decided to sell the estate.

Cameron couldn't afford to buy it, so sadly he had to give it up.

He had moved to Aberdeen when he was nineteen to attend King's College but the course didn't suit him, or more to the point he didn't suit the course.

University life was too much for him at that time in his maturity, so he ended up working at a local builders' merchant.

He'd lived a solitary life since then. A few girls had come and gone, but Cameron liked his own space too much and found it hard for someone else to invade it, and anyway why did women need so much stuff? They took over the bathroom and the wardrobes, he'd felt isolated in his own home by most of the ladies he'd dated. He had tried hard but in the end none of them wanted to settle down with a grumpy so-and-so.

He enjoyed his time at the builders' merchant and found that he could measure quantities out in his head without the need for scales or measures. He was popular with all the staff and especially the local builders, some of whom called him Cam, which he hated.

Thinking back now to his younger days at the croft, he had liked nothing more than lying out on the soft warm grass on a clear fragrant night, studying the stars. His favourite game was trying to work out angles between particular stars. His passion for maths, especially geometry, had led him to a degree course in maths at uni.

After leaving the croft for the last time, he had headed to Dundee and enrolled as a mature student on a physics degree. He adapted to physics like a 'grouse to the moor', as his grandpappy used to say. He sailed through his degree in two years rather than three and came out with a 2:1. He straight away enrolled onto a masters, which had led him to this spot in Cumbria.

His masters thesis title was 'Could Our Natural Water Resources in the United Kingdom be Better Used and Managed?'

He was mainly interested in whether a network of underground pipelines could be laid in such a way that water could be moved easily around the country, thus alleviating drought conditions and the need for water restrictions.

Farmers, growers and the tourist industry relied heavily on ready amounts of water. Global warming had definitely had an effect on climate change all over the British Isles, so a solution to avoid a national water crisis was needed.

His starting point was Loch Ness in Scotland, using a GPS system that could measure the thickness of a hair from space. This, coming from a satellite thousands of miles away, amazed him.

He had made his way around the loch, starting from its northernmost point. He'd worked his way around the whole expanse of water, taking water-edge measurements every half a kilometre. The recordings he was taking were geographically positioned and with elevation (height relative to each other) as well. All the readings went directly back to his iPad, onto a 3D mapping system set up especially for him by the IT bods in the university.

When he finally settled down to study his iPad it was a balmy evening in Dundee. It had taken him two days to map all around the great loch. He'd picked up his favourite, a freshly made Scots pie and chips, from Josie's Fish and Chip Shop on St Giles Terrace.

While eating, he tapped the screen of his iPad. The mapping app opened up, with all his readings there for him to see, in chronological order.

Slowly all the readings were automatically plotted onto the map, starting from the north. Two thirds down the southern side of the Loch and all had been going well, when suddenly the readings were turning red. Cameron studied the map closer and scratched his now balding scalp. This anomaly carried on all around the southern end of the loch and a third of the way up the northern edge, where everything returned to normal again.

Strange, thought Cameron as he studied the whole 3D map, all those damn red readings! Only one thing for it: he would have to go back and take all those bad readings again. He slept fretfully, dreaming about water monsters floating on large, colourful waterbeds. He woke with a parched throat, thinking he'd been shouting at the creatures to get off his loch.

Porridge with local honey for breakfast and he was out on the road before 7 a.m.

It was a long day but with the readings finally taken he headed back to his flat that evening, hoping this time they would show up green as the rest. His hopes were dashed as the same anomaly showed up again. Can't be, he thought. How is it possible the water level is higher on the southern tip of the loch than the northern? Every schoolchild knows that the surface of any expanse of water always stays level. What can be causing this? Come on, get your physics head around it. Gravity, yes of course – gravity, the phenomenon that holds everything down and creates order in nature. But why would there be less gravity at the southern edge of Loch Ness than the northern?

Maybe not less gravity but something beneath disturbing it.

Loch Ness is 36.3 kilometres long and the difference in level between top and bottom is apparently only a few millimetres, but it shouldn't be there, he thought.

*

The next morning, Saturday, he was sat in his favourite corner of his local bar, reading his newspaper, just a black coffee to accompany him.

'Seen it yet, then?'

Cameron started. Tomos MacLeish, or Tam as he was better known, has slid into the seat opposite. Born and brought up in Edinburgh, Tam had studied biology at the university and later became head lecturer in their science department. He looked across the table at Cameron with his old grey beady eyes.

'What? Seen what, Tam?'

Tam nodded towards the window. 'Out there, the beastie, Nessie, whatever they call it nowadays.'

'No,' said Cameron. 'Should I have?'

'Well, you're out there most days with your geo–thingy!'

'GPS!'

'Well? Have ya?'

'No!' Said Cameron, eager to get back to his morning paper.

'They only feed there, you know.'

'What? Who? What are you on about, Tam?!'

'Nessiteras rhombopteryx, that's what the renowned Sir Peter Scott called them.'

Cameron folded his newspaper noisily in an attempt to show Tam he was not amused at being disturbed.

'No sign of it, then?' Tam pressed.

'I'm not searching for any monster, Tam. I'm undertaking a technical survey of the loch to help with my thesis, that's all.'

'All's going well then?'

'Well ...'

'Ah! Ah, so you have found something. Come on, spill the beans.'

'Nothing to do with what you're thinking. It's just a hiccup in my readings, I'm sure the bods at the uni will sort it out.'

From the age of six or as far back as he could remember, Tam had been intrigued by the stories of the Loch Ness Monster. So, when in late 1987 the renowned Sir Peter Scott turned up on the loch with sonar, radar, whatever he was using, Tam had thought 'this is my chance' and if there was anything down there Scott was bound to disturb it, so with tent and high-powered camera and nothing much more he'd packed in his job at the university and headed for the great loch. That was over thirty years ago, and still nothing had been found or seen.

But Tam hadn't given up and had spent nearly every summer month since camped out around the loch, although in a bit more comfort these days having bought a camper van.

'I've always believed, as some did early on, that there is an underground passage somewhere out there to the sea,' said Tam, 'or better still, maybe into a large prehistoric undersea world.'

'Well, I'm not looking for passages or undersea worlds,' said Cameron, 'and if I did see anything I'd keep my mouth shut and my head down.'

'So, you don't believe in it, then?'

'No, sorry Tam, I don't,' he barked, opening his newspaper and getting back to the sports page, where he'd left off.

After Tam had left, something he'd said bothered Cameron a lot.

A large underground cavern – could this empty space be causing the gravitational anomaly? It would have to be big though, gigantic in fact, to have such an affect. That's a very Jules-Verne-esque theory so get it out of your head right now, Cameron.

So now here was Cameron, planning to do the same exercise a week later around the great Lake Windermere. It took just over a day to complete, Windermere being just over eighteen kilometres in length. After a delicious lunch at the Waterhead Coffee Shop on the northern shore of the lake, he set off back to Dundee.

All the way back he mulled over Tam's idea of this vast underground chamber under southern Scotland, full of water, containing all manner of prehistoric beings. Maybe old Tam wasn't as senile as Cameron had once thought. The underground cavern maybe … but prehistoric creatures? No way.

On returning to his flat he loaded the data he'd recorded into his iPad and as the data self-plotted onto his 3D map there it was again: red height readings all around the northern edge of the lake.

Now, this is getting silly, he thought to himself. Is there a gigantic underwater cavern deep beneath the earth's crust, spanning from mid-Scotland to northern England, or more likely two extra-large caverns maybe connected in some way by a long passage? This void under the earth's crust maybe formed when the continents as we know them today split apart from Pangaea and then filled with fresh meltwater from long-ago ice ages.

This was all getting too much for Cameron. He needed to get his head back to reality and get on with his work. After all, the university was sponsoring him to attain some sort of formula for his thesis. Maybe he could ask the IT bods to override the red readings and instead plot the same height reading all around the water's edge of both lakes. That would do it, and any thoughts of enormous underground prehistoric water-filled caverns could be left to future exploration – and Tam's dreams.

Buried Treasure

———⟨⟨◦⟩⟩———

Mohammad Ishmael was nineteen and lived in Luxor, Egypt with his mother and father and younger sister, fourteen-year-old A'isha.

His mother Abiha worked as a room cleaner in the nearby Hilton hotel, while his father Nasir owned a horse and carriage (a caleche), in which he transported tourists around the historical sites of Luxor most days.

Since the 'Arab Spring', a Western connotation of some uprising which Mohammad didn't fully understand, the reduction in the tourist trade in Egypt, Tunisia, Morocco and many more Islamic countries had caused a great downturn in their economies.

Both his parents had found it very difficult to keep themselves fully employed, and there were many days when no money came into the household.

Mohammad himself had completed his education three years earlier; he had wanted to continue but the plight of the family income made it impossible, he had to find some employment no matter what, to supplement the family income and protect his younger sibling A'isha from the troubles of the outside world.

Working as a street seller, Mohammad had sold perfume to provide money to cover some of the days his parents could not earn. He also worked longer hours than he declared to his father, which he was highly embarrassed about.

He knew how hard his father and grandfather had worked in providing for the future of the family, but since his grandfather had his stroke, his mother had taken it on herself to work (against all family tradition) but in a changing world as his father had said, needs must!

With his extra bit of money saved every week Mohammad finally had enough to buy something he had dreamt about: a drone (UVA); nothing too expensive, just one that was simple to operate and easy to fix if things went wrong.

Mohammad had read all about how drones might be the future, either in military, emergency services or for domestic use.

Every Wednesday and Friday a cruise ship would dock north of the city, and hundreds, if not thousands, of tourists would disembark. He knew his father would be busy both days and his mother would be needed in the hotel. It was on these days that Mohammad would take off on his scooter and ride out of the city over the bridge sixteen kilometres to the south towards the Valleys of the Kings and Queens. His quest was not these tourist attractions: he ventured further out into the Western Desert to a place that was quiet and with a flat landscape that stretched for miles. Perfect place to fly a drone, thought Mohammad when he had first ridden out there.

This day was a Wednesday in mid-April and the landscape was the same as when he had first set his eyes on it all those months ago in late September the year before.

His Uncle Abdul-Rahim, his mother's brother, had been killed in the 'brotherhood uprising'. Abdul had lived a solitary life with no wife or children to leave his possessions to, so it all fell to Mohammad. It was mostly the usual household bric-a-brac, and the only thing that had any worth was an old Vespa scooter. Mohammad thought it was brilliant and with his father's final permission he was allowed to learn how to ride it so long as it was well away from the street where they lived, busy traffic and most importantly his father's horse. This had in time led Mohammad out into the Western Desert, where he found himself now.

With a beautiful clear blue sky over the Western Desert towards Libya, this set the scene for a large oval amphitheatre a kilometre across by one and a half kilometres deep where Mohammad could hone his drone control skills.

This amphitheatre was a perfect place: high stone cliffs to the south and west with a shallow wadi to the east and north. In the centre there was a rather small circular mound about one metre high which Mohammad decided to use as a control point. After a few hours of playing around, he was very satisfied with the drone, and more importantly his control of it.

Mohammad set his drone down on the sand while he sat down on the mound and reached out for his lunch. Lunch today was stripped feseekh with sweetcorn in flatbread, wrapped in a muslin cloth. After eating, he laid back on the mound and rested, letting the heat of the spring sun warm his body.

He lay there and then wondered how this small mound had formed – was it created by the swirling khamsin winds blowing around the centre of this flat amphitheatre, or had something else formed it? He dug his right hand deep into the soft, gritty sand and found it was very easy to push his hand further and further in. He was down past his elbow when he felt something solid but smooth. He got to his knees and started to dig frantically, that smooth surface he'd felt intriguing him.

It was hot, and the little water he had brought with him simply wasn't enough for this hard work. He continued digging and thirty minutes later he could almost see the solid surface he'd felt earlier. He dug slowly and carefully and within minutes a flash of yellow emerged from the moving sand beneath his fingers. Frantic by then, he dug deeper and more yellow came into view. What had he come across? He just couldn't comprehend.

He looked up at the setting sun and knew he had to leave soon otherwise his parents would be worried. He left but determined to return another day with some equipment to help expose what he'd found.

Over the family evening meal his father declared that the cruise ship was staying in port for a day or two so he would be out early the next day. A'isha asked her mum Abiha what she was doing.

'I will be working too, praise be.'

*

The next morning, A'isha left for school just before eight o' clock, so Mohammad gathered the tools he needed for the task ahead.

When he got to the site, thankfully it was in the same condition he'd left it in the night before. He quickly got to work with the shovel he'd brought with him, making the excavation a lot bigger. He worked slowly and carefully, aware that the limited amount of water he had carried with him had to last. After two hours of hard digging he had exposed a circular gold-coloured surface two metres across. What was it, and was it really gold? He decided to take a section a metre wide and dig down to expose what was below the dome. By late afternoon he had exposed the two-metres-wide section and had dug down two metres deep. The surface of this thing was so smooth it was almost mesmerising. Mohammad was now very excited by his find but worried that it was so big he could not possibly expose this thing on his own.

That evening, after the evening meal he knocked on his sister's door.

'Yes?'

'A'isha, can I talk to you?'

'Of course, come in.'

Mohammad explained everything to his sister.

'What should I do?' said Mohammad.

'Well I'm no expert in Egyptian archaeology, but I think you've discovered something very important. Only last week in school we were discussing in a history lesson the folklore of a golden pyramid. The great pyramid builders lived in the eighteenth dynasty, around four thousand years ago. Well, we know the great pyramid at Giza was once covered in white limestone, and who knows, with maybe a golden top.'

'Do you think this thing I've come across is a buried pyramid?'

'Who knows?' said A'isha. 'What you should do though is contact the authorities.'

'A'isha, the thing is covered in a golden substance. If it is gold, what I've exposed alone could make us very, very rich.'

'Yes, it could, my lovely brother, but if it is what we think it is, it could make the *whole of Egypt* rich. Which would you prefer?'

'My sister, you are very wise. Hopefully one day you will be a politician. This great country needs people who think like you.'

*

The next day Mohammad arrived at the Luxor Museum on the Kornish Al Nile and asked to speak to the resident curator. Wassim Alib, a tall man with greying hair at the temples, strode into the visitors' area with confidence and authority.

'Well, young man, what can I do for you?' he said.

'I think I might have discovered the Golden Pyramid,' said Mohammad nervously.

'Really? And what makes you think that?'

'THIS,' said Mohammad, showing him a picture of his dig on the screen of his phone.

'My God, is this real? Where is it?'

'Out in the Western Desert,' answered Mohammad.

'Can you take me there?'

'Can you ride scooter!?' said Mohammad with a wry smile.

'Perhaps in my vehicle, then,' said Wassim.

Two hours later and they were both standing at the site of the original mound.

'This is incredible,' said Wassim. 'We need to cover this up for now and keep it secret. Can you do that, Mohammad?'

'Yes, for this great country I'll do anything.'

'Well done. Our great country is in a precarious political situation at the moment. It might take a while, but with the right people involved this find could make Egypt great again.'

'Thank you, sir,' said Mohammad.

That evening, after the family had eaten, Mohammad announced that he was thinking of taking up the chance of a sponsorship to embark on an archaeology degree in Cairo.

'Well, this has come as a complete shock,' said his father.

'Are you serious?' said Abiha.

'I think it's a GOLDEN opportunity,' said Mohammad, with a sly wink to A'isha. A'isha grinned back.

'Are you two cooking up something?' said Nasir.

'No, nothing, Father. I just feel that Egypt's sands have a lot to deliver up, not only to us but also to the wider world, that's all.'

'We can't stop you going, son, but who's going to pay for it?'

'Don't worry, Father. There's a small government bursary set up for aspiring young archaeologists.'

'We had no idea you were interested in the subject,' Abiha said.

'It's something I've longed to do for a while, and now I've got the chance I feel I should go for it. One day, Father, you'll have a famous archaeologist and a prominent politician to be proud of.'

'Hopefully I'll live long enough to see it,' smiled Nasir.

Mirror Mirror

———◦☺◦———

James McCarthy woke very early. He was twenty-six years old. It was just past six o' clock, not his usual time to be awake. He took a long gulp of water from a tumbler on his bedside cabinet and tried to get back to sleep. He tossed and turned for over an hour and then finally gave in and got up.

He lived alone in a three-storey terraced house constructed mainly in red brick, but the topmost floor was constructed of timber frame painted black, with white infill panels. His bedroom was on the top floor – he felt safer up there. James had lived in the house alone since his mum had died four years previous.

He dressed and made his way downstairs. As he plodded to the kitchen, something was troubling him – a dream he'd had during the night just didn't make any sense. He tried to recall it, but he just couldn't piece it together in his mind; never mind, he thought, probably nothing anyway.

He made himself tea and toast and walked into the lounge.

It was a cold Saturday morning in late October; not a work day, so he could relax. He sat down to enjoy his breakfast, but something felt strange – first he thought he was being watched! Looking round the room, his eye caught the large mirror over the fireplace.

The reflection back from the mirror wasn't his room: it resembled the room in shape, but there was a very ornate wallpaper and part of a picture that he didn't recognise.

He stood up and walked towards the mirror. Now he could see clearly that he was looking into another room. He studied it more closely: the furniture and furnishings were old, very old in fact. He tried to fix a date – maybe Georgian or early Victorian.

Looking directly into the picture, he noticed a mirror on the wall opposite over the very fireplace he was standing in front of. Strangely, he could see himself looking into the room from the opposite wall.

He stepped back. Whoah, this isn't happening, he thought. He looked again and, yes, it was all still there. But that's my reflection opposite, he thought. As he moved his head sideways, the image in the mirror across the room did the same.

He stepped back again, thinking hard. What was happening here? Firstly, he thought, well, mirrors always reflect back the image that's facing them, then he thought, if this mirror was very old, could it be reflecting an image it had seen from very long ago?

He tried to work out what he was seeing, and finally he surmised that this virtual room he was looking at was actually located somewhere between the face of the clear glass and the reflective surface at the back of the mirror.

He stepped forward to take a better look. He could work out that this reflective room was the same room he was now standing in but an image from many years ago. The furniture was old, like he'd seen on the *Antiques Roadshow*, and the walls were covered in a highly embossed wallpaper, and there were lots of paintings of people and some landscapes.

As he watched, someone walked into the room. It was a maid dressed in a black blouse and long black skirt, white apron and white mob cap.

She bent down at the fireplace and started to prepare it for lighting later. It took her quite a while, cleaning and polishing.

James was mesmerised by her. Was this someone who lived in this very house over one hundred and fifty years ago? But that can't be!

He stepped back and studied the old mirror hanging over the fireplace. It looked very old: it had a timber gold guilt surround, the decoration was mainly leaves and some seashells, from what he could make out. There was some slight damage to the surround, and the mirror plate had brown spotting, showing its age.

The mirror had always hung there as far back as he could remember. Who hung it there, he wondered – was it his parents or did they inherit it? Had it always hung there since the house was occupied?

James decided to leave it for a while. This was all a little bit strange and disturbing. He decided to go for a walk and then call into his local football club and watch the home match scheduled for that afternoon.

He got back to the house around six o' clock, having picked up fish and chips on the way.

Curiosity took over, so without switching a light on, he crept into the lounge and looked in the mirror.

The other room was still there. The fire was now glowing bright and an elderly gentleman was sat in the open armchair, close to the hearth. He had a distinctive handlebar moustache with the ends wound up tight which he was twiddling with his left hand. He wore a blue embroidered smoking hat with a dark blue tassel and a thick plum-coloured paisley patterned housecoat tied at the waist with a pure white silk rope, with tassels.

He had cloth slippers on his feet, and on his right ankle a white bandage was visible. Gout, thought James.

He looked well-to-do, maybe a doctor or solicitor. He was smoking a long white clay pipe; he leant forward and tapped the contents out on the side of the fireplace. He then took a small round tin from his housecoat pocket, flipped the lid as if he'd done it a thousand times before, then with his thumb and fore-finger he picked something out of the tin, lifted his hand to his right nostril and sniffed. He then repeated this with his left nostril.

Snuff, James surmised.

A large glass of red port stood temptingly for him on the low table to the left of the fireplace.

He looks well looked after, thought James. I wonder who's doing that? James left the old man to enjoy his smoke and snuff.

He entered the kitchen and emptied the contents of his fish and chips package onto a plate. He opened his laptop on the kitchen table and looked on the internet for his property. Various options of maps of his street popped up in the search results.

What he was looking for was a date maybe. The gentleman's attire and demeanour suggested to James this was the early Victorian, in fact soon after the Georgian, period – he was thinking around 1840s, maybe. He found an old town map and saw that Magdalene Terrace in his street was built in 1849.

That fits, he thought to himself. The elderly gent looks well into his sixties so would have lived most of his life through the Georgian period, which would account for his dress and demeanour.

After finishing his meal, and satisfied he'd hopefully tied down a date, as he walked back towards the lounge he wondered if that mirror really had been hanging there all this time.

On entering the lounge, he could see that the mirror and its surround looked very heavy, too heavy to carry perhaps. Maybe that was why it was left?

He looked in the mirror again: this time there was someone else in the room with the elderly man – a much younger man. He was dressed in a black frock coat and he held a black cane with an ebony handle in his right hand. The pair were obviously in deep discussion about something.

James watched them; then he felt ashamed that he had been watching them for so long.

He was about to stop when the discussion seemed to be getting more frantic, and James felt a tension building up between the two. The older gentleman stood up to confront the younger, and for some reason the younger gentleman raised his cane, perhaps in some way to protect himself, but the older man was frail, no match really.

On seeing the aggressive move by the younger man, the older gentleman flinched, stumbled back and fell. James stood on tiptoe to see where he had fallen.

He saw him lying prostrate, his head close to the

tiled fire surround. The younger man lowered his cane and bent down, lifting the old man's wrist, feeling for a pulse.

Suddenly, face pale, he got up and quickly left the room.

My God, thought James, what have I just witnessed? Not a murder but something akin to it. He hoped the younger man had gone to get help, but after nearly five minutes of waiting he could only suppose that the younger man had left the house.

A few minutes more and the maid walked in. Seeing her master, she flung her hands up to her face and fled the room.

The vision in the mirror slowly faded and James was now looking at the familiar surroundings of his lounge, although now his room felt very different to him.

He went to bed early but failed to get to sleep, and as he lay there he resolved to find out in the next few days who these people were and what had happened after the elderly gent had died.

He thought the local library would help, as perhaps the parish records could establish who lived in the house all those years ago. Something was still troubling him though: there was something, an object on the low table to the left of the fireplace close to the glass of port.

James prided himself on his photographic memory, something that had got him through college without too much trouble as he could instantly recall any page of a textbook, which meant he didn't need to spend endless hours revising for an exam: it was all there in his head.

He closed his eyes tight and took himself back to the room. It took a while but soon the image appeared in his head, and there he could see it – an engraved glass bowl. That's it, he thought. The engraving was of the Crystal Palace. Of course – the Great Exhibition, which people from far and wide went to visit in 1851. I wonder, is this my date? Well, at least it gives me a start.

Of course, the census – there would have been a population count in 1851. Now he knew he might be getting somewhere, he finally managed to get to sleep.

James took the Monday afternoon off work, saying he had an urgent doctor's appointment. He made his way to the local library and looked online, finding an ancestry site, bringing forth the death certificate of Richard James Wilson, retired solicitor. *Misadventure,* it read.

Perhaps they thought the port, his gout and the snuff all contributed to his demise. There was no indication of who the younger gentleman was, and a seemingly unrelated family was living in the house by the following census, ten years later.

The head of this household might be the perpetrator, but James had a feeling he was not.

Next James tried local newspapers, all on microfiche at the library. He had a date to start – any time after the Great Exhibition. It didn't take long and there, just over a year after Richard's death certificate, a report on the death of Edwin James Wilson. The report read:

Second Death Befalls House
in Magdalene Terrace

The nephew of the previous owner, Mr Richard Wilson, who tragically died in the house a year earlier, was found dead in suspicious circumstances.

Mr Edwin James Wilson was found by his housekeeper on Wednesday evening of this week. It is believed that Edwin Wilson had been walking in the countryside on the afternoon of that day, as reported by his housekeeper.

The post-mortem revealed he died of poisoning by a certain kind of mushroom. The housekeeper proved that she had not cooked for him that day so was absolved of any blame.

It was assumed that Edwin had picked a mushroom that afternoon and in some way ingested it.

James made his way back to the house, satisfied with his recent discoveries but concerned that the mirror might still hold more information.

On entering the house, he looked in the lounge but could only see his room being reflected back.

Perhaps now I've learned of these events, the mirror will be satisfied and not reveal any more, James thought.

He made himself a sandwich and mug of tea and walked into the lounge to relax.

He froze. The mirror was now showing the other

room again. He shakily placed his meal down and stood looking in.

He watched as someone came in, and he could now make out who it was at once – the nephew Edwin, although he was now in some kind of distress. He staggered into the room, clutching his stomach tightly with both hands. He dropped to his knees, then slowly pitched forward and lay motionless on the floor.

Suddenly the maid walked in – the one from the vision earlier, the one who was making the fireplace. She was dressed differently now, though – she looked like the housekeeper, or maybe even the cook.

She purposefully walked into the room, stood over this prostrate figure, then bent down and visibly uttered a few words close to this gentleman's ear.

Then she stood once more, turned away from the prone figure, pulled the clip from the back of her head and shook her long brown hair until it cascaded down over her shoulders, and walked out of the room. On her way, she glanced furtively at the mirror, and James was sure he caught a very slight smile on her lips as she passed out of view.

The view of the room gently faded away.

Beekeeper

———❦———

Jason Strong had recently enjoyed his fifty-eighth birthday, the highlight of which was a surprise party, organised by his wife and three daughters which had brought all his brothers and his sister together for the first time in almost twenty years. It was held at a local spa hotel, so everyone booked in with their spouses for a weekend of relaxation and fun.

Frank, the eldest brother, had spent all his career since university in local government as a planning inspector. James had been in the fire service, just as Jason had but not quite for as long, and Anna, the only girl, was a midwife at the Lincoln County NHS.

George, the youngest, ran a smallholding in mid-Wales, stocked mainly with sheep but also his beehives.

Jason had spent most of his adult life in the fire service, joining when he was twenty-one and retiring at fifty-five, with thirty-four years' service under his belt, of which he was very proud. Getting to the rank of Station Commander was the apex in his life, only overshadowed by the birth of his three daughters and four grandchildren.

Retirement, to some, was a difficult time: loss of friends and work colleagues, the banter and comradery that filled their everyday lives.

This was not the case for Jason though: he wanted

to explore life and all it had to offer. He had attended too many RTAs (road traffic accidents) in his work life to ignore how devastating maiming and loss of life could be to families, and how short life could be.

He was immensely proud of his three daughters; they had made their life choices well, in work and in their partners. These unions had produced four grandchildren to date – two boys and two girls. Only one, the youngest, of his daughters had got married, much to the relief of himself and his wallet.

This lovely late August morning, and Jason was on his way to the allotment, he could just feel the hint of coolness in the air; autumn was on its way. The allotment was only a five-minute walk from the house and contained all manner of plants and vegetables he'd planted but most of all his pride and joy, the beehive.

His excursion into the world of allotments had surprised him. He'd only been discussing the chance of growing his own vegetables with his mate Ray down the Golden Lion one winter's night a couple of years before when in early spring a local plot became available, and with the forthright Ray having put his friend's name down for one a few months earlier.

Jason was no great gardener; he'd learnt a lot from the other allotment growers: how and when to plant potatoes, sow spring onion, carrot, leek and lettuce seeds. Most failed, but he did provide the household with enough – salad stuff, tomatoes, sweet peppers, cucumbers and lettuce – to keep Lucy his wife happy for him to spend as much time as was practical at the allotment.

He'd been married to Lucy for thirty years and in fact they had spent a fortnight in the Caribbean to celebrate May 5th, a date imprinted on his mind. Such a happy wedding day, Jason and Lucy had been childhood sweethearts in secondary school and had drifted apart due to career paths and had both found partners that eventually didn't work out; then, on a school reunion a few years later, they had found each other again.

Lucy was a staff nurse in the NHS. Jason admired her commitment to her work and patients from the time they had met. Accident and emergency was a different world from the wards of surgical, medicine etc. Lucy loved the face-to-face world of A & E, never knowing if the next patient was a cut finger or a heart attack.

Jason unlocked the gate to the allotments and re-locked it on entry, a crazy situation, he thought, for who would want to steal vegetables? But surprisingly, some do.

Mark was there as usual; he had the plot next to Jason.

'Lovely morning,' said Mark.

'Yes, looks like a few more to come.'

'Better get watering, then. Those runner beans of yours are crying out for water.' Mark always had a critique to pass on; he'd had his allotment the longest – twenty-one years. Anything and everything had past Mark's way over the years, and what he didn't know about allotment growing wasn't worth knowing.

What Mark didn't have, and what was to Jason's advantage, was the beehive.

'They've been really busy this morning,' said Mark, nodding towards the hive.

Having a beehive and managing it was a crazy notion to most of the population, but Jason had been led into it by his younger brother, George.

George's small holding was near a village called Llanelwedd, just north of Bwylth Wells. George had been a beekeeper for many years, gaining notoriety for producing some of the best honey in his locality and selling it at the local farmers' market. At his fifty-eighth birthday party back in May, Jason had got into a long conversation with George about bee keeping and its benefits – not only to the countryside but to man's survival on the planet. George had twenty-five beehives, but the exact number in use could vary up and down, depending on winter weather conditions, the age of the queens and proper management of the hives. George was satisfied if only two or three hives were lost over the winter; he knew he could make the numbers back up over the summer months.

Jason had become fascinated with bees after his long discussion with George at his birthday treat. George had suggested a small hive to start with and then to let it grow as a natural enhancement to the allotment. Jason had to put his proposal forward to the Allotment Keepers' Society. Thankfully they were very supportive, although the interview was fraught, as Jason had to remember all that his brother George had coached him on regarding beekeeping.

Finally, after major discussions between young and old on the Allotment Keepers' Society the vote went four for and three against.

Jason was delighted but nervous because now he had to take on all the intricacies of bee keeping to a personal level. He read about it as much as he could, but first-hand knowledge was the best, so a trip to mid-Wales for a whole weekend was arranged with his brother George.

May and June were the best months of the year to learn about beekeeping, after the stagnant months of the winter, when early spring wakes up the hive and the pollen is brought in by the surviving workers to feed the new brood, which means the queen was well and active. The hive suddenly comes alive in April, and by mid-May the queen is producing hundreds of eggs every day. By early June a hive, in a good year, could be supporting 20,000 bees so by mid-July, if you've avoided a swarm, then a hive could contain up to 40,000 bees. Impressive – and to watch this spectacle was one of Jason's favourite things. Bees are mesmerising to watch, with the workers going in and out, doing their job, bringing in nectar and pollen.

'Those bees aren't any good for your runners, mate!' said Mark. 'You need a good heavy bumble bee to pollinate them. Honeybees can't get into the flower, but when a bumble bee lands on the outer petal the flower opens up for them to feed.'

'Interesting,' said Jason. 'I didn't know that.'

'Yes, if all the honeybees die out, as is being predicted, we might all be surviving on runner beans alone,' said Mark with a little chuckle.

'Marvellous thing, nature. How after millennia flowers, bees, insects, moths and butterflies have adapted so that some will only work with one and not the other,' said Jason.

'If honeybees die out, it might take another millennium for others to adapt, and we haven't got that time, so take good care of your little friends in there,' Mark said, nodding towards the hive.

'It's the queen I need to protect the most, Mark. Only maybe a few thousand bees will survive the winter, but they will do everything to protect her.'

After checking around the allotment and pulling some young beetroot and picking some runner beans and peas, Jason left – but turned at the gate.

'I'll be back in the morning with my gear, to check everything's alright in the hive. Just warning you, as they do get a bit jittery when I'm disturbing them.'

'Just bring your smoke puffer thing, that always keeps them docile,' said Mark with a thumbs-up sign.

*

The next day was bright with a gentle breeze, a good day for checking the hive. The whole colony would be busy, so most would be out foraging on the local flora, be it mostly bramble flower at this time of year.

When Jason got to the allotment Mark was waiting for him at the gate.

'You need to see this,' said Mark. 'I trapped it this morning. It was sunning itself on my shed door when I got here. Luckily, I had a glass jar handy.'

Mark held up the jar, and Jason took a step back.

'What the heck is that?' exclaimed Jason.

'Well, it looks like a type of hornet to me, but its size and colouring are all wrong!' replied Mark.

'My God, that's big!' said Jason. 'I've read about certain hornets being destructive to honeybee colonies. Hopefully this is not one of them!'

'Well, when you get back home, check it out on your internet thingy, with a picture. I'm sure someone will identify it.'

'I've got to check out my hive today,' said Jason. 'If a queen egg is due to hatch then the old queen will take off with half of the hive to set up another colony – thus a swarm.'

'Okay,' said Mark. 'I'll keep this little beauty for the rest of the day, but you know my feelings on wildlife.'

'I do,' said Jason. 'Please don't release it until I get back to you.'

'Better hurry. Karma says I can't keep it for more than a few hours.'

*

Jason was on the internet as soon as he got home, straight to his laptop in the study.

'What do you fancy for lunch, dear?' was Lucy's shout from the kitchen.

'Anything, darling. I'll be with you in a minute.'

Scrolling through hundreds of photos of hornets and killer wasps, nothing added up to the picture he now held of the creature in the jar. My God, thought Jason, is this a new species?

Jason was affiliated to the Lincolnshire Beekeepers Association so he put a message on their blog:

New(?) species of hornet recorded today; picture attached. Colour predominantly green but with purple sections on its abdomen approximately 40mm long. Found close to my hive in Hedgestone Allotments. No sign of attack but will keep close watch over the next couple of days.

Paul Thomas, president of the Lincolnshire Beekeepers Association, saw Jason's message on their blog and he himself put out a message.

*To all Lincolnshire beekeepers and beyond, please keep
a look out for an unusual hornet, picture attached, any
sightings contact me ASAP.*

*

After a lunch of prawn salad and a slice of Lucy's
home-made apple pie, Jason made his way back to the
allotments. Mark was waiting.

'I can't keep this thing indefinitely. Have you iden-
tified it or not?'

'No, I haven't,' said Jason. 'Looks like it's a new
species, which will take ages for to officially identify.'

'Do I let it go?'

'It will be on your conscience, not mine,' said Jason.

Mark unscrewed the lid and let the creature fly
away.

'Sorry Jason, but you know my stance on "all creatures"!'

'Let's hope you haven't let a real "cat out of the
bag".'

Jason pulled his full beekeeping suit on, gloves and
all, and set about checking the hive. He used a bit of
smoke from his galvanised steel smoker box but not
enough to completely subdue the hive and returning
bees. His mind was still on Mark letting the hornet go!

The hive was in good condition: the sections were
full of honey and there was no sign of young queen
eggs, although he did notice the start of a queen egg
capsule on the side of one section – but no larva
inside.

Later that evening Paul rang Jason.

'Jason, it's Paul from Lincolnshire Beekeepers.'

'Hi Paul, what can I do for you?'

'The hornet – what are your plans for it?'

'Well, nothing. It's been released.'

'What! Why did you do that?'

'Ah, well, I didn't catch it, my allotment neighbour Mark did, and he's a practising Buddhist, and he was compelled to release it.'

'My God, do you realise what he might have done?'

'I did chastise him, but he was adamant.'

'Well, it now looks like we've got a 24/7 scenario on our hands, and that means keeping a round-the-clock watch on all hives in the area.'

'If it happens again and my neighbour has it in a jar, next time I'll have a large net ready!' Jason reassured him with a slight smile.

'Anything wrong, hun?' inquired Lucy as her husband ended the call.

'Hopefully not. We have a rogue hornet in the area which might be attacking beehives, so we have to be extra vigilant from now on.'

'Oh, that's dreadful – and I was so looking forward to tasting your honey this autumn.'

'I'm sure we'll be okay. The hornet is too big to get in the hive anyway, and we're only surmising it's a danger. It might be quite the opposite.'

On the local ten o' clock news that night, the last item showed the picture Jason had taken of the hornet and the request put out that if the hornet was seen it should be reported straight away, a direct telephone number to Defra appearing on the screen.

*

It was again a warm, calm morning a couple of days later as Jason made his way to the allotment to check out the hive. Mark was there as always – 'bright-eyed and bushy tailed', as Jason like to imagine him.

'Any news on the hornet?' asked Mark.

'No, none at all, and very worrying for the local beekeepers, including me!'

'I see yours are a bit subdued this morning,' said Mark.

'Not surprised with a "released hornet" on the loose!' Jason emphasised the 'released'!

'I've been reading up on hornets,' said Mark.

'Have you now?' replied Jason. 'Are they as bad as we beekeepers make out?'

'Yes, and worse, although the honeybees have a way of protecting the hive by surrounding the hornet and smothering it, although this leaves a lot of casualties.'

'That's life!' replied Jason. 'They are protecting their queen. Maybe next time, if there is a next time, you'll let me handle it.'

'Fine by me, but you know my faith – if I catch anything, I'll let it go.'

Jason put on his protective suit. He wanted to check on the queen egg he'd seen started a few days earlier. He too noticed the activity in the hive was subdued.

After checking all of the sections in the hive he noticed a small beam of light shining in at the back of the middle box. After further investigation he found a hole about 4mm across at the back of the hive. His first thought was that a hornet had got in, but the hole was too small for that. Something had affected the activity of the hive though – what could it be?

He carefully checked the base of the middle compartment and found an empty egg casing, coloured green with purple segments.

No, he thought. That damn hornet had eaten its

way into the back of the hive and laid an egg. When was this, he thought to himself. Maybe before Mark caught it, so giving the egg time enough to hatch and now disrupt the hive?

I need to find the queen and fast, thought Jason. He carefully lifted all of the sections out one by one, but the queen was nowhere to be seen. He did notice, though, a larva in the queen egg case he'd found before, which was a good thing, meaning a new queen was about to hatch. More worrying was he couldn't find the resident queen or the young hornet either. He placed the trays back in, but the section with the young queen egg he placed in a brood section on top of the hive with a division plate in between. His thinking was if the young hornet was replicating the workers or one of the drones in the hive then it might be a little bit larger so wouldn't be able to get through the slot in the division plate. That led to another scenario: what if the young hornet had replicated the smell and size of the queen? It could well be producing hundreds of young hornets under the guise of the hive queen! I need to find the queen now, thought Jason as he slowly took the lowest box apart, checking all the sections one by one.

To his sorrow and anger, he finally found the queen with a red dot on her back, dead at the bottom of the hive.

'I have to destroy this hive straight away,' said Jason.

'You can't do that,' replied Mark. 'What evidence have you got?'

'It would take too long to explain; I plan to do it this evening when all the bees have returned. Hopefully I have a young queen in the top section, with enough workers and drones to start again.'

Jason rushed home and put out a message on the Beekeepers Blog, explaining as best he could what he'd found in his hive.

After dusk that evening Jason returned to the allotment. First he removed the 'brood box' on top. He then subdued the hive with lots of smoke, sealed it up and moved it away from its location near the hedge. With a heavy heart he poured petrol over it and stood back as he lit a match tied to a length of cane. Whoosh, up went the hive, and Jason's hopes as a beekeeper with it.

At least he had a small section with a young queen and enough bees to start again.

Within two weeks, three beekeepers had reported to Paul, confirming Jason's description of a small hole in the side or back of a hive. All had been destroyed.

*

Christine Blake was a keen amateur entomologist and had set up a long net across open parkland, hoping to catch and record butterflies, moths and any insect that happened to stray her way. She'd set it up very early in the morning and planned to remove it before the park got busy with people. She checked it every fifteen or so minutes.

'Now, what have we got here?' she said to herself as she checked her net for the last time that morning before taking it down. 'You are a pretty thing, aren't you? Let's put you somewhere safe so I can get a better look at you later.'

She checked her identification chart at home – no, nothing similar to, nor anywhere near, the recorded wasps and hornets on her chart. 'Mmmm,' she thought. 'You must be the one all the recent fuss has been about. Quite a celeb you've turned out to be!'

Christine emailed Defra immediately and received an email back by return. 'They have asked me to keep you secure and someone will call by to collect you later. I'm going to call you Freda in the meantime, or perhaps a Latin name, maybe Vespa Crabro Lucidus.'

'All I hope is that you haven't caused too much damage and disruption in the local area while you've enjoyed your recent freedom. Wherever you're from, hopefully we'll be able to get you back to either your homeland or the institute you might have escaped from!'

Tepee

———◦◦◦◦———

Grey Wolf sat all alone watching the funeral pyre burn furiously until it finally, with a ghostly groan, collapsed in on itself. As the flames shot higher, he swore he saw his grandfather, White Elk, lift gently into the sky.

Grey Wolf turned his face to the sky and gave out one long loud howl, as if to help White Elk on his journey.

Running Deer, his father, came and stood in front of him, holding out his hand. They gripped each other's wrists and Grey Wolf lifted himself up into his father's embrace. They walked away, Running Deer's arm over his son's shoulder. Running Deer was now head of their tribe.

All of White Elk's possessions had been burnt with him, a ritual of the tribe. Falling Leaf – Grey Wolf's mother – was now busy moving all of their possessions into the old chief's tepee. Grey Wolf would now have to take his parents' tepee as his own, and soon he would also have to take a wife of his own. First, though, to furnish his tepee with his own furs and animal trophies; now he had to hunt using all the skills White Elk had taught him.

Taking up a position in the centre of his newly acquired tepee, Grey Wolf dropped to his knees and lifted his head up to howl, something he'd done forever when he was stressed or felt danger. Looking directly up through the hole high in the tepee roof, he was looking straight at the Great Bear – a good sign, he thought; I must hunt tomorrow.

He settled down on his straw bed and pulled a single blanket over himself.

I will need good strong, warm pelts before the winter snows come, he thought. I only have two new moons before then.

He fell into a restless sleep.

What his grandfather taught him was to know your enemy, where he lives and hunts, and avoid contact as best you can. The great big grizzly bear and the wolf pack were the most feared.

The wolf pack and their territory were well known to the tribe. The pack would never risk attacking the village, but they would always be on the lookout for a lone brave out hunting.

The grizzly was much more unpredictable, especially the young males, who would wander aimlessly around. The camp had had a few encounters over the years with a lone male barging into the village looking for food.

He was up before the sun the next morning. He ate some corn mash he'd cooked, filled his pouch with dried buffalo meat and berries. As he walked away from his tepee he looked across and signalled to Running Deer which way he was heading and for how long – three days he hoped.

With his bow and twelve arrows in his quiver slung over his back, he left the camp at a steady pace, running down the path which led away from the camp and then right and up into the forest. The undergrowth was lighter up there, so it didn't slow his pace.

The first day was just travelling, moving as far away from the camp as possible. By late afternoon he had found a spot to camp for the night. He walked out about thirty to forty paces and then did a complete circle around his favoured spot. This manoeuvre allowed him to pick up any trails or even sleeping animals close by whom might give him some trouble during the night. Other than a few small rodents scurrying away from his silent footfall he was satisfied he was alone.

It was a warm night; he didn't need to light a campfire, so after eating he settled down for the night. He was soon fast asleep, but soon awake again – it felt like early morning, but he knew he hadn't slept for long. A noise had woken him; something barging its way through the undergrowth, heading straight towards his small camp.

He stood up, lifted his bow, placed an arrow, the tip on his left hand, and drew the string back and took aim. This thing was getting closer and closer. It wasn't charging but rather just seemed to be walking slowly but purposefully towards him. As it got close, Grey Wolf calculated its size and aimed for its chest. He stood his ground, heart pumping but totally focused, just as White Elk had taught him.

Finally, this creature burst through into the clearing not ten yards in front of him. It was an Elk, a majestic one, totally white with huge antlers. The Elk stopped and they both stared at each other, neither wanting to move. Suddenly the Elk's form started to change very subtly: first the antlers disappeared, then it shrank and changed into a form Grey Wolf knew so well: his grandfather.

Grey Wolf dropped his bow and made a move towards his grandfather, but White Elk raised his hand to stop him, then gestured to sit down.

Grey Wolf did as he was told, then his grandfather sat opposite him and smiled. They talked about hunting and where Grey Wolf should travel the next day to find the best deer and beaver to hunt.

Soon, Grey Wolf got tired and fell asleep. When he woke it was early morning and the sun was up, a little bit later than he wanted to wake, but where was his grandfather? Not a sign. Did he dream it? He checked where the Elk had entered the clearing: no disturbance in the undergrowth at all. Very strange, he thought, but his meeting with White Elk was so clear in his mind it must have been real.

He packed up his camp and headed in the direction he had discussed with his grandfather.

Minutes later, he had come to the top edge of a steep valley; he decided to follow the edge for a while before heading down. He could see a rocky outcrop a distance in front of him. Some instinct inside him told him to stop, and as he did so a magnificent stag walked with purpose from out of the forest and stepped up onto the rocky outcrop.

Grey Wolf's heart missed a beat. He dropped to one knee and carefully lifted his bow over his shoulder and reached back for an arrow. The stag hadn't seen him nor smelt him on this still summer's day.

Grey Wolf manoeuvred himself towards the edge of the forest and, staying low, he made his way forward. When he was within thirty feet of the animal he waited until the stag bellowed again.

He then remembered his grandfather's wise words: 'Don't take down the strong specimens of the herd, you want them to keep the herd strong and healthy for the future. Take the weaker ones. That way, you sustain the herd for generations to come.'

Looking at this magnificent stag, now he understood what his grandfather meant. He lowered his bow and watched the stag scrape his front hoof on the rocky outcrop numerous times, then with one last bellow it turned and walked back into the undergrowth it had emerged from.

Grey Wolf walked carefully over to where the stag had stood, his moccasins barely making a sound on the rough terrain. The spot the stag had chosen, the rocky outcrop, was on a bend in the valley; it was a good place as he could clearly see for miles up and down the valley. The stag's bellow would have been heard for a great distance, a warning to other stags, no doubt. With the vision of the magnificent stag in his mind – forever, he was sure – he made his way forward along the edge of the steep slope.

He had made his way a few hundred yards further along the valley edge when a movement away to his right made him drop to one knee instinctively. He crept forward – a small copse of bushes was blocking his view, but it gave him good cover too. Then he saw them: about twenty deer, mostly female with a number of young fawns alongside, some still feeding from their mother's milk. A couple of young bucks made up the group; these bucks kept to the rear, and a large older female led them.

Grey Wolf studied them for a while, a plan forming in

his head – which of the herd to take down and where. The herd now walking across an open area of ground was not the ideal spot to attempt anything, he needed them to go to a spot where he could plan an ambush.

He noticed the doe at the head was leading them towards a group of pine trees. If he could get there first, he had a good chance of a kill.

He stepped away and made his way back to the valley edge, then slipped down the steep side but kept his footing well. The valley gave him good cover; he could move quickly without being seen. He travelled a measured distance then rose out of the valley. He was now well ahead of the herd and far enough away. Keeping low, he made his way around and into the small group of pines. The herd were still some distance away, grazing as they walked, which gave him enough time to camouflage himself.

First he reached up into the branches to gather as many young pine cones as he could. Crushing them between two stones produced a small amount of liquid from each one, which he rubbed vigorously over his body. Then, using some old pine branches laying around, he quickly constructed a small hide. He was ready now; all he needed was the herd to come within firing distance. He set up three arrows in front of him; he was sure he wouldn't get the chance to release any more.

He breathed in and out slowly to reduce his heart rate and to stop himself shaking. His adrenaline was on overload.

The herd was approaching. The lead doe was doing a wonderful job, although she hadn't realised the danger she was leading the herd into.

Grey Wolf had chosen his target: a lone female to the rear of the herd. She had no fawn with her so no other animal to trouble him after he had struck. A fawn would stand by and maybe try to defend a fallen doe, and he wanted the rest of the herd to run away.

The lead doe was now passing his hiding place. He only had a minute or two now. His posture was good; he had a clear line of sight. His muscles straining, he released his first arrow. Without looking down, he put another arrow in his bow and fired it. The first arrow struck the doe in the side of her neck – it had gone deep into the flesh. The second also struck her neck but lower down and not so well bedded.

The herd scattered, and even the injured doe took off. Grey Wolf picked up the arrow he hadn't used and strung it into his bow, ready. Leaving his hideout at an even pace he followed his quarry. He knew the first arrow would be doing its job and weakening the doe. He was right: only a few hundred yards ahead of him and the doe had stopped running and was now staggering along. He kept a distance behind; even a weakened animal would put up a strong fight to survive, and he didn't want to get injured way out here by a kick or from a swipe of an antler.

The doe finally fell to her front knees and then rolled over onto her side. Grey Wolf pounced on her and with his hunting knife in hand he slit her neck open. The doe's eyes were wide open in fear. As she took her last breath, he held her tight around the neck, lifted his head and howled. He prayed that her passing wouldn't be wasted. She would provide good meat and a warm pelt for the future.

He rolled her onto her back then skilfully, with his

sharp hunting knife, he expertly gutted her then, slicing through the top vertebra at the back of the neck, he removed the head. Then he set about skinning the animal, something he'd watched and helped his grandfather do many times. After cutting free the choicest of the strong red flesh from the rump and shoulders, he placed them down on the laid-out skin. After folding the skin over the meat and tying it all together, he lifted the bundle onto his shoulders.

He needed to get away from this spot as soon as he was able. Darkness would soon fall, and the wolf pack, out hunting, would pick up the scent of the kill. After gorging themselves on what he'd left, they would surely follow his scent to get the remainder of the kill.

Grey Wolf was young and strong. He walked through the night, hoping he would make enough distance between himself and any wolf pack. He reached the camp just after midday the next day.

He walked over to his father's tepee and laid the bundle out on the ground in front of him. Running Deer stood and embraced his son, then he signalled to a family sitting outside a tepee not far away. A young girl rose up and walked towards them. She was no more than fifteen years old.

'This is White Dove,' his father explained. 'She arrived at the camp yesterday. Her village has been attacked, and she was the only one to get away.' Running Deer laid all the meat out on a low wooden rack close by. 'I will divide this between all of the families, but first you must have your share.'

He cut off a chunk of meat from the largest piece and laid it down on the deer skin. Grey Wolf picked up the skin and handed it to White Dove, bowed his head towards his father, and turned and walked towards his tepee. White Dove did the same and followed a few steps behind.

Grey Wolf took the skin and laid out the meat for her on a large flat stone slab in front of the tepee entrance. Not a word had been spoken between them, but they both knew instinctively what to do.

Grey Wolf took the skin. He needed to scrape it clean, cure it, then let it dry in the sun. The whole process would take a few days.

White Dove, on the other hand, had lit a fire outside the tepee and had cut numerous strips from the chunk of meat for drying. The rest of the meat she had cut into chunks and it was slowly boiling away in a cooking pot over the fire when Grey Wolf returned.

While they were eating, Falling Leaf walked towards them, carrying a large grizzly bear fur. She walked into the tepee and laid the large fur over the raised wooden bed, then returned outside, nodded to them both and walked away.

After finishing their food, and with the sun slowly setting over the hills far in the distance, they walked together into the tepee. After White Dove had settled on the bed, Grey Wolf walked outside. He fell to his knees and looked up at the full moon, a loud howl emanating from his throat. When he had finished, he looked at the millions of sparkling stars looking down on him. He knew then that this would be the last time for a long while he would need to howl. He walked back in, lay down on the bed beside White Dove and without a word spoken he wrapped the large fur around them both and fell fast asleep.

Shell Cottage

—◦◦◦◦—

Peter was twelve years old and lived near the Lincolnshire coast with his parents, Sue and Carl, and younger brother Harry.

It was Saturday morning and Peter was outside on the rear patio, cleaning and oiling his bike. It was late January – a dull, overcast day but hardly any wind. His bike was just over a month old; if he didn't look after it no one else was going to – a lesson learned from his grandfather.

'Hurry up! Lunch is nearly ready!' Sue shouted through the kitchen window.

'Be there now, Mum. Nearly finished.'

'So, where are you going this afternoon?' asked Carl as they finished off their lunch.

'Just out to the coast and back. Shouldn't take us long.'

'Just be careful on those narrow roads. There's far more traffic now than there was in my day.'

'Yes, Dad, we'll be careful. It should be fairly quiet, not many tourists about this time of year.'

'Okay, dear, just don't be late back. Four o clock will be plenty. It gets dark soon after.'

'Yes Mum. See you later.'

He had arranged to meet up with his best friends Roger and James to go for a cycle ride together. They planned a short ride out to the coast, just over three miles away. James lived just around the corner from Peter so they had arranged to meet there. When Peter rode up to James's gate Roger had already arrived.

'Come on, slowcoach. Been oversleeping again?' quipped Roger.

'Thanks for that, Rog. No, in fact I was up early, oiling my bike.'

'Come on you two, stop squabbling and get going. We haven't got all day.'

'How's United doing? I see they've got Arsenal this afternoon?' Roger asked James as they rode off.

'Good at the moment. Hopefully we'll make Europe again this year,' he replied.

'Stop chatting, you two, and peddle. We want to spend some time at the beach, don't we?' Peter admonished them.

Still chatting, the trio rode off in the direction and on the route they had planned in school the day before. As James had quipped, if you go down, you have to come back up again – that's bike riding.

They had now cycled for about twenty minutes. The sky was still heavy and overcast, keeping the road surface wet. They rode through a slight blanket of fog and came out the other side into a much brighter day. They came to a cottage with a young girl leaning on a green garden gate. *Shell Cottage*, the white sign read.

'Are you going to the beach?' she shouted as they rode slowly past.

Roger stopped. 'Yes we are. Is it far now?' he asked.

'No, not far. Just don't be too long. The tide comes in very quickly nowadays,' she said.

They thanked her and waved as they rode off.

'I'm Sally,' she shouted after them.

'Peter.' – 'Roger.' – 'James,' they shouted back.

A few minutes later and they were leaning their bikes against what looked like an old timber mooring post. They made their way down to the shoreline, picking up handfuls of pebbles on the way.

'My dad calls this "duck and drakes",' said James as he skimmed a stone across the water.

'I've heard it called that too. Wonder why?' questioned Peter.

'Did you see that one?' asked Roger. 'It flipped right over that wave.'

'Right, let's count how many bounces we can get. Most is the winner,' encouraged James.

They lost count of the time until their pebbles had run out.

'Right!' said Peter. 'I think we should be getting back. You know what that girl said.'

'Sally,' replied Roger.

'Yes, her, at the cottage gate. She warned us about the tide here. Come on, let's go.'

'By the way, I think I won with fifteen,' exclaimed James.

Collecting their bikes, still arguing whether James had actually got fifteen or fourteen, they rode back past the cottage.

'Glad you've taken my advice,' said Sally as they passed.

'Yes, thank you,' replied Roger. 'See you again soon.'

Back through the mist they rode.

'Funny how the air feels damper and darker again now,' Peter mused as he noticed that the road was wet again.

'Seemed different back there!' Roger agreed.

'Yes, I felt it too,' James replied.

They were soon back at James's house.

'What's the time?' asked Roger as they pulled up outside the drive gates.

'Three thirty-five,' said Peter checking his Fitbit, 'and we've done just under seven miles.'

'Great, I'm ready for my tea now,' replied James. 'See you both in school on Monday.'

Peter and Roger rode off in opposite directions, waving as they went.

Peter put his bike back in the garage and locked the door as he left.

'How was it?' asked Sue as he walked into the kitchen.

'Great' was all he said as he passed through into the lounge.

'How's the Boro doing, Dad?'

'Down one nil at the moment but plenty of time to go. How was your ride?'

'Great, thanks. my Fitbit says we did almost seven miles.'

'What? It's only just over three miles to the coast from here. Checked it many times in the car.'

'Well, that's what it says – look!' He showed his dad the screen.

'That thing must be faulty. We'll have to send it back. Must still be under warranty, I should think!' said Carl.

'Well, we took the direct route, straight there and straight back,' he replied.

'Well, that's almost half a mile more than you should have done, that's all I'm saying.'

'What's all the raised voices about? The Boro not doing well, is it?' questioned Sue.

'No, Mum. Dad reckons my Fitbit is faulty!'

'How come? You've only had it a month!' she exclaimed.

'I set it up properly this morning for our bike ride, so if it says we did just under seven miles, I believe it.'

'It's only just over three miles to the beach from here. Even taking the detour to James's house there's no way you've done almost seven miles!' demanded Carl.

'Anyway, how was your ride? No mishaps, I hope?' asked Sue.

'Everything was fine, the beach was lovely and we took heed of the girl at the cottage not to be too long.'

'Really? What girl? What cottage? There's no cottage on that road that I can remember. Are you sure you went the right way?' asked Carl, still wondering about the seven miles.

'Yes, Dad. Perfectly sure. The cottage with the big oak tree on the side and a red front door, I remember that. The girl's name was Sally. She was about our age, although come to think of it I haven't seen her in school!'

'There's definitely no cottage on that road, son. Maybe before the big storm in 1953, but definitely not one since. I've lived here all my life – and that's a long time,' Carl said, smiling.

'Well, we did see it, and we all spoke to her,' Peter replied.

'Never mind, come and have some tea. It's all laid out on the kitchen table – cheese and ham sandwiches, your favourite.'

As Peter and Sue headed for the kitchen, Carl was deep in thought.

Did they really cycle that far? Maybe there was a cottage, oak tree and a girl? But not for a very long time; he was sure of that.

The Swing

Jenny Secombe was an independent, private lady, sixty-eight years of age. She had taken the train down from Temple Meads station in Bristol, England, to Carmarthen in West Wales. From there she had taken a twenty-minute taxi ride to this spot where she now stood in the village of Llansteffan on the west side of the Towy estuary.

She remembered the village so well, having spent many happy childhood holidays with her mum, staying at her Aunty Lynne's house.

She walked down Water Lane toward the beach and the play area that she had such fond memories of. It took her a few minutes as she walked from the taxi drop-off point; she reminisced, seeing herself in that lovely blue frock with white trims to the hem, cuffs and neck. Her mum had bought it for her, especially for that holiday, and she wore it every day.

She reached the play area, still with happy memories set in her mind; the swings, seesaw and roundabout were all there, just as she remembered them. Still daydreaming about times long past, she could see her mother sat on the little wooden bench in the sunshine, knitting as Jenny spent many happy hours, especially on the swings.

The swings looked a lot smaller now. The last time

she had set eyes on them was in the late fifties when she was maybe nine years old. Auntie Lynne had moved away, so they'd never returned.

She remembered vividly swinging as high as she could and listening to her mum, shouting to be careful.

Jenny sat on the seat, her slim figure easily nestling in between the now rusting chains. She gently swung to and fro, looking out over the slow-flowing murky waters of the estuary. She remembered the fresh cockles, the taste still residing on her papillae as her tongue traced around her dry mouth.

She kicked harder on the swing, feeling confident. She wanted to go as high as she could remember. Higher and higher she went until she reached as far as she could safely go. She swung back, eyes closed, and at the highest point she was suddenly nine again, leaning back, arms straight, looking up into a clear blue sky.

She swung forward, exhilarated by the whoosh of air through her hair and the tingle in the pit of her stomach. As she reached the top of the forward swing, eyes still closed, she was fourteen again, Tom Davies stood there, beautiful, handsome, blond-haired Tom. With a smile that would break any girl's heart, he put his hands out towards her. She wanted to grab them again, but she swung back.

Now at the top of her back swing, she was twelve years old on her first day at senior school, the start of a beautiful seven-year journey.

Forward again and at the top another vision: now nineteen, she was dancing in the arms of Geoffrey, her betrothed, smiling and giggling together. Meeting in the first year of university, it was love at first sight for them both.

Back again and she was sixteen now, head bowed, watching a tear fall slowly onto the beautiful polished pine coffin that held her beloved dad. Such a sad day.

Forward again and she was twenty-four now, walking down the aisle in pure white, to Geoffrey, so handsome in his morning suit. She looked right, hoping to catch a glimpse of him again, but no.

Back the full length of the swing, eyes still closed tight, she was eighteen, leaning out of the train window, waving madly to her mum, left behind on the station platform, off to university.

Forward and she was twenty-six and looking down into the eyes of her first-born, Julie, the most beautiful thing she had ever seen.

Back the swing travelled again and when it reached its zenith she was twenty-one, looking at the bright blue stone in the solitaire engagement ring on her finger.

Forward now she kicked. She was thirty-two now, on a sun-kissed beach in the Seychelles with Geoffrey, Julie and little James. That was a lovely holiday, one of the best ever, she thought as the swing recoiled and took her back to twenty-eight and to the birth of her son James. Geoffrey was so proud.

Forward again. Now she was forty-five, finding that first lump in her breast, staring in the mirror, seeing the strain again on her face, thinking of the horror to come.

Back the swing took her to a happier time, thirty-six, to watch again James take the lead role in the school nativity play.

Forward now and she's fifty, looking well and smiling, a meeting with the oncologist, receiving the good news of remission.

Back again now to forty-four, tears streaming down her face as Geoffrey drove back from the university campus, now home for the next three years for her beloved Julie.

Forward now to a sad time her – mum's funeral. So many people came, making it a special but sad day. Jenny was now sixty.

The swing took her back one last time to James's passing out parade at Sandringham. She was fifty-one.

Forward now – the one she was dreading – seeing her darling Geoffrey laid out in the funeral home, so peaceful.

The swing now slowed, allowing her to open her eyes, back to reality. She stood as the swing stopped. She thought back; it had been a good life. She walked away, not looking back, forward to the taxi to take her back home.

She passed a sign, half-hidden, lying in the under-growth. She paid no attention to it. Her mobile rang. It was Julie.

'Mum, where are you?'

'I'm fine, dear. Just on my way back.'

'Back from where?'

'Oh, you wouldn't know. I won't be long, be back before it gets dark.'

'Gets dark?! I thought you'd gone to the shops?'

'A little bit further than that, dear, but I'm safe and well. See you later.'

A strong breeze blown in from the estuary parted

the undergrowth covering the sign to reveal its contents. It read:

This play area has been closed and all equipment
removed for health and safety reasons.
Sorry for any inconvenience caused.
Carmarthenshire County Council, 1999.

Wicket Cottage

⸺❦⸺

Allan MacManus had recently bought a small thatched cottage in the Chilterns. He was thirty-five and single, and the sale of his watercolour paintings was his main source of income.

His main reason for moving out of the London suburbs to the Chilterns was especially for his paintings. He liked the ever-changing weather conditions, the freshness which brought total shifts in the feel and colours of the area from day to day.

He was sat in his lounge; it was an open-plan layout that took up the whole of the ground floor including the kitchen of this late-Victorian cottage. An open spiral staircase led upstairs from the dining area to two bedrooms, one now his studio, and an en-suite bathroom. A large stone open-fire chimney breast took up part of the far gable wall, with a large black iron dog grate taking up a good proportion of the opening. I'm going to have to source a good supply of logs to keep that thing going over the winter, he thought.

He was happy with the property he'd recently bought; he'd dreamt of an English cottage garden and this property had it all: a climbing rose covering the front of the cottage with a small front garden filled with standard roses, peonies and delphiniums. The natural thatch roof finished it off for him.

It was an early summer evening and he had just finished his meal of dressed crab on a salad base with crusty white bread. A full glass of white wine in his hand, he laid back on his green chesterfield settee and studied the room more closely. The proportions were as he expected but something was nagging in his mind. With all the experience he had of drawing landscapes, something in this room didn't fit with the outside.

It was a late June evening, hot and balmy, so he decided to check the proportions of the cottage and got up and walked outside.

He checked the dimensions from the right-hand gable to the first window, and all looked in proportion. From the window to the middle window (originally a door) and then to the end window, all was as the inside. The distance from the far-left window to the outside gable wall looked longer than the lounge inside. Intrigued, he went back inside, and yes, he could see now the distance to the wall on the right of the farthest window was so much shorter than what was depicted on the outside.

He tapped the white plastered wall to the left of the stone fireplace: it sounded hollow. He found a long, thin screwdriver in his work box and carefully made a hole close to the fireplace. He pushed the screwdriver in slowly but firmly, and it easily made it past the plaster and then into a void behind.

Is this possible? thought Allan. The agent's details didn't show any hidden rooms.

Captivated, he made the hole a little bit bigger, then he took out his mobile phone from his rear pocket and flicked the light on. He could now see into the void. It looked deep – even deeper than the outside wall had offered.

Why, he thought, would someone block this up? it would give a whole new dimension to the lounge if it was cleared.

I'm not going to investigate tonight, he thought. I need tools and covers before I start ripping an old lath and plaster wall apart.

The following morning after breakfast Allan had everything laid out ready. He made the hole from the night before bigger, then using a saw he carefully cut down and across until he had a hole a metre down and two metres across to help investigate further. Kneeling on the floor and using the light from his mobile phone, he pushed his head into the void and looked around. He could see down to the floor – same level as the lounge – and back, deeper than he expected, but when he looked up, he could see nothing, only what looked like a dark wooden shelf. The walls side and back were also covered in the same dark wood.

Using his saw, he cut up but couldn't get past the shelf. Not wanting to damage it he made a new hole above the shelf and cut in with his saw, then slowly cut upwards.

After a half a metre he stopped and cut across for half a metre, like below, and then down and then across to make a neat aperture where he could look in.

He had exposed part of a beautiful old dark oak bookcase. It looked like the sides and back of the void were lined. There was another shelf above, so now carefully and deliberately he set about removing all of the lath and plaster wall covering this abandoned alcove.

When all was removed, the uppermost shelf was just at his eyeline, so he stood on tiptoe to peer over the edge of the shelf. There was something on there, so he grabbed a stool and stood up to get a better view. Laying on the shelf there was a cricket bat and ball covered in dust. They looked very old, especially the ball.

Why were they here? Who'd left them there?

He picked up the bat and ball and stepped back into the room. He studied the ball more closely: very old, he thought. He threw the ball up into the air. He held out his hand and was about to catch it again when suddenly he found himself standing in the same spot in this very room but with different furnishings all around him. He caught the ball.

The room was a lot smaller and the furniture looked antique.

'Come and zip me up, will you, and put that bat and ball back on the shelf. Brian would be livid if he knew you'd picked it up.'

Who, what, where am I? thought Allan.

'Come on, Tom, or you'll be late for the game.'

Tom! Who's Tom?

'Tom, stop daydreaming and help me, would you. Your match starts at three and it's quarter past two now,' said this very slim woman, now stood in the doorway with her back to him.

Allan/Tom did what he was told and helped fasten up the back of her summer dress.

'Right, go on, have a good game. I'll be watching!'

He didn't look back.

Outside the front door, leaning against the cottage, were two bicycles, one gent's and one lady's. He set off as if somehow he knew where he was going.

The cricket ground was a mile and a half away. It was a glorious summer's afternoon, and the hedgerows were full of colour as he cycled along this narrow country lane with its patches of bluebell, red campions and a few early foxgloves, then in a dip in the road some wild garlic, its scent hanging in the air as he zipped through.

It took him just under fifteen minutes to get there; plenty of time to get padded up and out onto the square.

Tom always opened with the captain. A good crowd had already gathered, the ladies in their fine white dresses and flower-brimmed hats, the gentle-man in their straw boaters and waistcoats. The pavilion was open, and someone was serving lime water for the ladies and beer and wine for the gentle-men.

Allan headed straight for the changing room door. He wanted to avoid any contact until he'd figured out where he was – and who!

The changing room was empty, much to his relief, so he quickly got padded up, picked up his bat and headed out towards the crease.

'Someone's keen!' someone shouted from behind. He didn't look back, just lifted a hand in acknowl-edgement.

A few moments later, another shout came from the pavilion veranda: 'Show them how it's done, Brian!'

Brian! Allan turned to see a very portly gentleman striding out across the grass towards the opposite end of the crease.

Was this THE 'Brian'?

'Come on, lad, look lively!' came a shout from Brian at the other crease, and again Allan raised his hand in acknowledgement. He studied Brian more closely: he was much older, dark slick hair combed back from a high forehead, black eyebrows over a pair of beady strained eyes, a full dark moustache under a bulbous nose and rosy red cheeks, late thirties or early forties, Allan guessed. Not a handsome man, thought Allan, but someone who held respect and admiration; a military man, he guessed.

He was to take the first ball; the opposing bowler had taken up a spot about thirty yards behind the umpire. Wow, thought Allan, a fast one, is it? Can I remember how to do this, even? I haven't played cricket since my school days.

No time to think as the first ball screamed down the pitch towards him. He blocked it and it rolled maybe ten yards away towards backward short leg.

'Run!' came the shout from his opposite partner, so he did, and as fast as he could. As they passed on midwicket, captain Brian dropped his bat and swung it hard, the leading edge catching Allan squarely on the shin.

Ouch, he screamed in his head, not wanting anyone to know – especially the opposition. He ploughed on just reaching the crease in time.

Why did he clout me? thought Allan. Was it an accident? A steely glare from opposite gave him the answer.

With that, the opposing bowler was passing by Allan's left shoulder. A flash of his arm and Allan watched as the ball pitched mid-wicket and turned away to the right. His partner took it cleanly on his bat, but not well – the ball glanced off towards short leg.

'Run!' Again, the shout from the opposite end.

Allan knew this time it was futile. First he had a very sore leg, he had to avoid his adversary and make the opposite crease in the short time the chap at short leg had to pick up the ball and hurl it at the stumps.

Amazingly, the chap missed, and Allan made it.

They survived until the end of the over, and a new bowler was called up.

This gave Allan a chance to wander down the wicket, tapping out divots with the bottom of his bat as he went. Halfway down, he met his partner.

'How's the leg?' was all he said.

'Fine, no thanks to you!' replied Allan.

'Oh, don't be like that. Take it like a man … as you've taken my wife!'

'What? What did you say?'

'You heard,' he said as they made their way back to their opposite creases.

This new bowler, at the opposite end, walked halfway down the pitch, measured Brian up with menacing eyes, then turned and glared at Allan as he passed. Intimidation, thought Allan; a weak sign, if ever he saw one.

The bowler took an age to walk back to his mark. God, where is he going, Allan thought, out of the grounds? Brian, to be fair, stood his ground, patting his bat firmly on the turf to show he was ready. Suddenly a flash past him and the bowler struck, a full-length yorker clear under his opposite number's bat and the bails flew high into the air.

'How's that?!' came a chorus from the opposition fielders.

A scowl in his direction and his adversary, as he now liked calling him, made his way back to the pavilion.

The rest of the match went well. Allan ended up as top scorer with a credible forty-seven. His team won the match and they all made their way into the pavilion. Now for the tea and cucumber sandwiches, thought Allan.

His imagination was well below the offering spread out on the long table in front of him: there was beef, salmon, salad, cheese and tomato sandwiches of varying sizes, all laid out neatly over trestle tables covered in crisp white tablecloths.

Allan found himself sitting opposite his 'adversary' and presumably his wife sitting on his right – a strikingly handsome woman, short brown hair, icy blue eyes and red pouty lips to die for. He remembered the hair and dress from the cottage but not much else. What was I doing there, in the cottage, thought Allan. Is Brian right? Am I having an affair with his wife?

As he tucked into his second salmon sandwich he felt a foot – he assumed it was someone's foot – stroking up the inside of his left leg.

He didn't move. He looked across the table and caught a slight wink from the beautiful creature opposite. Oh god, perhaps I am!

With that, a clink of cutlery on glass and someone spoke further up the long, beautifully laid out table.

'I call on our courageous captain, Brian Smart, to say a few words. Not forgetting today that he and his lovely wife Valerie are celebrating their fifteenth wedding anniversary.'

Brian pushed the last piece of his cucumber sandwich into his mouth as he rose to speak. He just stood there for a second, not moving, then his hands gripped the edge of the table as his eyes bulged and his face got redder. He started to claw at his throat as he slowly sank to his knees. Valerie screamed.

Someone shouted, 'He's choking!'

Someone else cried out, 'Hit him on his back!'

A gentleman sitting next to Brian bent down and hit him square between his shoulder blades with the heel of his hand. This didn't help it only made matters worse for Brian, as he was pitched forward, striking his forehead on the edge of the trestle table.

As all this was happening, Allan had leapt out of his seat and was rushing around the end of the table to get to Brian as soon as he could. Everyone was now standing up, the ladies with their gloved hands to their mouths. Someone was comforting Valerie.

Allan reached Brian. He bent over him, brought his arms down with hands gripped together just under his rib cage, and he lifted him up with a gigantic tug upwards.

The offending piece of cucumber flew out of Brian's throat and landed in a wineglass further up the table.

Brian gasped for breath, sank to his knees again, coughing loudly.

A big cheer went up around the room and then spontaneous applause broke out.

Allan quickly made his way back to his seat with lots of back-slapping and clapping. As he sat down, he looked across at Valerie. 'Thank you,' she mouthed at him.

The vice-captain took over with the speech duties, and a cold compress was rustled up for Brian's forehead. Allan rubbed his sore shin and looked across at dishevelled Brian. Hmm, perhaps karma does work, he thought.

At the end of the afternoon, and with the sun still fairly high in the sky, Allan was out on the veranda, leaning on the rail. Someone quietly stood beside him – he looked to his side to see Valerie.

'Thank you for what you did earlier. Whatever you did saved my Brian's life. I will always be in your debt,' she acknowledged.

'Don't say that. It was nothing really, I just acted on instinct.'

'How's your leg?' she questioned.

'I'll live! how did you know?'

'I saw what he did out on the wicket. I told you I'd be watching!'

'Why did he do it?' Allan questioned her.

'Well, he knows about us. He's not happy with the situation, but poor Brian can't see to my needs in that department. That's where you come in!' she replied as her right hand squeezed Allan's left buttock.

'Don't!' he said. 'People are watching.'

'Oh, don't worry, most here know what's going on anyway, that's the problem with village cricket clubs – everyone knows each other's business, and don't look shocked, there's a lot worse going on compared to what we're doing. Brian's got bridge club tonight so I'll expect you around seven?'

'Are you sure? His head is very sore.'

'Oh, he'll go if I tell him he has to.' With a quick slap to his rear, Valerie strode confidently from the veranda.

*

Seven in the evening, with the sun finally setting, as a blackbird called to its young from a mulberry bush opposite, Allan knocked on Wicket Cottage's front door.

The door opened to reveal Valerie standing there in a beautiful white and cream silk nightgown.

'Come in,' she said seductively and led Allan straight upstairs to her bedroom. She didn't share a bedroom with Brian; she allowed him his pipe and cigars in the lounge, but she had her treats upstairs.

As they stood by her bed, with just one movement of her hand Valerie's nightgown fell effortlessly to the floor. Allan was mesmerised by her slim naked body.

'Don't look! Act!' she demanded.

Allan pulled off his shirt but struggled with his belt. She jumped on the bed, grabbed him with both hands around his waist and pulled him towards her.

They fell on the bed, laughing.

Their lovemaking was good and satisfying.

'That was good!' she proclaimed.

'For me too,' Allan lied.

'Right, come on, out you go. He'll be back soon.'

Allan had never felt so used, but he completely understood.

He dressed, walked to the door, stopped, looked back at this beautiful woman stretched out on her unkempt bed.

'Go on!' she demanded.

'What would you do if I wasn't around?' he asked.

'Oh, there's been plenty before you and there'll be more to come. Don't think you're a special one. For now, you satisfy my needs. Now go.'

Allan tiptoed down the steep staircase, but before leaving he turned and walked into the lounge. The bat and ball still intrigued him, especially the ball – it looked so old. He reached up and took it from the shelf, felt its crease and the soft leather.

He tossed it in the air, held out his hand to catch it . . .

Sword Cottage

⸺◦❂◦⸺

Gethin Williams was a student at Aberystwyth University, studying archaeology. He was in his flat at his hall of residence, making a bacon sandwich, when his mobile beeped an incoming call.

He looked over at it: it said 'Mam Calling'. He pressed the 'Accept' button.

'Hi, Mam.'

'Hi, cariad, how are you?'

'Good thanks. Is everything okay?'

'Just to let you know we've got an official-looking letter in the post today, addressed to you. Shall I post it on, or open it for you?'

'Oh, go on, open it. I bet you're dying to know what's in there.'

He heard paper ripping on the other end of the phone.

A slight pause.

'Are you still there, Mam?'

'Yes, I'm here, just reading it. It's from a solicitor's office in Builth Wells, asking if you'll attend a reading of your late great uncle's will.'

'What! What great uncle? I didn't know I had any great uncles.'

'Neither did I, cariad, neither did I. It says you have to attend on the twentieth, which is next Tuesday. Can you make that? We'll come and pick you up, of course.'

'Umm, yes, I think so. I'll have to check when I have lectures, but I'm sure it won't hurt if I miss one.'

*

Monday afternoon and Bethan and Jim were walking along Aberystwyth seafront, waiting for Gethin to arrive. They saw him approaching in the distance and waved and pointed in the direction of the car.

After the usual hugs and comments about how thin the lad looked, they got in the car.

'Have you found out anything about this great uncle I've suddenly got?' Gethin asked from the back seat.

'Well, only that he might be on your father's side and he lived somewhere up on the border, not far from Ludlow.'

'Is he Welsh or English?'

'We don't know exactly, but a distant aunt who is still alive reckoned he lived this side of Offa's Dyke.'

'That's okay then. Have you found out a name yet?'

'No, but the old aunt thought it might be Arthur.'

'Well, we'll find out tomorrow, hopefully.'

'How's the digging going anyway?'

'It's not all digging, Mam, there's lots of theory too.'

*

Tuesday morning and Gethin and Bethan were sat in the solicitor's office, waiting to be seen.

'It doesn't look like there's anyone else coming. Perhaps he had no close family,' Mum said.

Suddenly a door opened.

'Mr Gethin Williams?'

'Yes, that's me.'

'Follow me, please,' said this rather tall gentleman with greying hair and a slight limp on his left leg.

'Please be seated,' he invited them both. 'And you are?' he asked Bethan.

'I'm Gethin's Mam. Is it alright?'

'Fine by me. Is it okay with you?' he asked Gethin.

'Yes.'

'Good. Then let's get on. I'm Geoffrey Davis, solicitor to the late Arthur Pendragon Williams, your great uncle.'

'Never heard of him,' said Gethin.

'Shhhh,' Bethan admonished.

'Well, apparently your great uncle knew a lot about you and especially your love of archaeology. In his will he leaves all of his estate and possessions to you, Gethin Williams.'

'Wow, am I to inherit a few rusty old artefacts, then?' Gethin questioned.

'Much more than that. Arthur had some land and a cottage a few miles south of Welshpool just on the Powys/Shropshire border. It's called Bwthyn y cledd – Sword Cottage is the best translation in English. It stands on approximately twenty-two acres of land.'

'Really!'

'Yes, and from this day forward it's all yours – enjoy. We hold the deeds; do you want them, or would you like us to keep them on your behalf?'

'Mam, what am I to do?'

'Well, accept it first, then we will have to sort out how to manage it.'

'Thank you, Mr Davis. Can you copy the deeds for me please, and keep them here if that's okay. Did you know Arthur well?'

'Not at all really. He came in last year to make his will. Other than that, no, I didn't know him. I'll have my secretary copy them for you before you leave. Oh, just a minute, before you go, there is a sealed envelope addressed to you too.'

Gethin accepted the envelope. He and his mam both shook hands with Geoffrey Davis and left the office.

'What are you going to do?' Bethan asked.

'Well, if you and Dad aren't busy tomorrow perhaps, we could take a drive up there and find out where this property is?'

'You have an address, do you?'

'It will be on the deeds, and I'm hoping more will be revealed when I open this envelope later.'

*

'So, what did the letter reveal?' questioned Bethan later that day.

'Quite a bit really. Apparently, he's got a cat call Lance and fifty or so sheep. From there, he rambles on a bit!'

'Go on. I'm intrigued,' demands Bethan.

'Well originally the cottage was called Bwthyn y llyn – Lake Cottage – because many years ago, and I'm thinking we're talking a long time here, there was a lake covering most of the land and further afield.'

'It sounds nice. Why change it?' questioned Bethan.

'I'm coming to that – give me a chance, Mam! Well, apparently, this lake was special. On certain evenings in the year, with the right light, the surface of the lake seemed to be covered in a myriad of small rainbows. He rambles on about King Arthur and a sword that was thrown in.'

'Excalibur?'

'Now you're being drawn into this silly story,' Gethin admonished.

'What else did he say? Did he look for it?'

'He did get a guy in with a metal detector, but all they found was an old bowl, which Lance now feeds from.'

'Is that all?' asked Bethan.

'Yes, and a note where to find the cottage key.'

'What a strange story. A shimmering rainbow lake. Does sound like something out of the tales of Arthur.'

I wonder if he was christened with Pendragon as his middle name, or did he just add it? thought Gethin.

'Well, let's sleep on it and see what tomorrow brings,' reassured Bethan.

The next morning, they found the gateway to Bwthyn y cledd and drove up a narrow, rough stone track, Jim driving very slowly as he didn't want to cause any damage to his car way out here.

'Goodness, it's just a shepherd's hut!' exclaimed Jim.

'It was fine for Uncle Arthur; it will be fine for me,' stated Gethin.

'You're not living in that!' exclaimed Bethan.

'Only joking, Mam.'

They found the key where Arthur had it hidden. Gethin opened the door and it creaked its welcome as they trooped in. No sign of Lance; out hunting for mice, Gethin thought.

The interior was very haphazard, as was perhaps expected for someone of an advanced age living alone. It consisted of two rooms only – to the left a small bedroom and right a living room/kitchen.

'Well, this will take some sorting and cleaning,' said Bethan, running her finger across the top of a small table propped up against the cottage wall.

'Hello!' came a shout from the front door. 'I'm Fran Jones. I live in the neighbouring farm just across the way.' She pointed to the west.

'Yes, come in, come in,' invited Gethin.

'I'm Gethin Williams, and this is Jim and Bethan, my mam and dad.'

'Just to let you know, I've been looking after the cat and the sheep for you.'

'Yes, thanks for that. Do I owe you anything?' questioned Gethin.

'Goodness no, happy to help out. Arthur was a quiet old soul, kept very much to himself, was a bit of a dreamer but harmless enough.'

'How long had he lived here?' asked Gethin.

'All his adult life, I believe. He inherited it from his grandfather.'

'What about his stories, and was there really a lake here many moons ago?' asked Bethan.

'We believe there was. The lower part of the land here, along with my land, gets very wet when we have heavy rain. It's the silt from the bottom of the so-called lake. Poor drainage, you know.'

A black and white cat suddenly appeared around Fran's legs.

'Ah, here's Lance, come for some food no doubt. He has it in the old bowl outside. He never stayed in the cottage, much preferred to sleep in the small stone outbuilding in amongst the bales of warm hay.'

Fran poured some dry mix into the bowl outside.

'What about water?' asked Gethin.

'Ah, that all comes from the natural spring outside. It runs all year round, never known to dry up!'

'Is it safe?' inquired Bethan.

'If you boil it well first,' Fran replied. 'Anyway, I must be off; got sheep to check. See you all soon, I hope. Bye.'

Gethin waved Fran off and stood outside his new front door surveying his newly acquired estate. He noticed the cat bowl by his feet: it did look very old and was engrained with dirt. This could do with a good clean, he thought. He brought it inside placed it in the sink and poured some water in to try to soak the ingrained dirt off. He found a scourer under the sink behind a dirty curtain hanging on a length of twine. After a good clean he could see this old bowl was more intriguing than he thought. There seemed to be an inscription running around the inside of the bowl just below the rim. It was very worn and difficult to see and read.

'Come on,' said Jim. 'Time we were getting back.'

'I need to pop back later if I can, Dad. Can I borrow the car?'

'Yes of course. Just go slow up that terrible drive.'

When Gethin returned later he brought with him some of his archaeological equipment. He picked up the old bowl, filled it full of the natural spring water outside and set it down while he prepared his equipment. The sun was setting behind him and for a brief second something caught his eye – something reflected off the water in the bowl.

He bent down to get a better look and there he could see it: a rainbow lying on the surface of the water.

Amazing, he thought. A complete freak effect of light and reflection. He used his brushes to thoroughly clean the inside of the bowl. It looked bronze but without proper testing he couldn't confirm. He then dried it, took a piece of butcher's paper and a coloured crayon from his bag and proceeded to do a rubbing on the inside of the bowl. He knew someone who would be interested to see it.

*

Huw Morris was a retired lecturer from Aberystwyth University and in his day a leading expert on the 'Old Welsh' language. Although now in his mid-eighties, his mind was still keen, and he kept in close touch with the university. Gethin knew where he lived so very gingerly knocked on his front door.

'Yes, who is it?' came a shout from inside. 'I'm not opening if you're selling anything!'

'It's me, professor. Gethin Williams from the university.'

'Well, why didn't you say so in the first place! Don't hang around out there, you're letting my heat escape!'

They shook hands and then Gethin followed him into his nice warm lounge. Too warm for Gethin but he thought, goodness, I might be like this one day!

'Well, what have you brought me? I see the cardboard tube under your arm.'

Gethin carefully pulled out his rubbing and let the professor unfurl it.

'Now, what have we here, lad?' Huw asked.

'It's a rubbing, sir, and—'

'Yes, yes, I can see that,' Huw butted in, much to Gethin's frustration.

'It's taken from the inside of what looks to me like a

bronze bowl. It's very worn down with age. I hope I've been able to get enough for you to decipher?'

'Why didn't you bring the bowl?' inquired Huw.

'A long story, sir.'

'Well, at first glance it's a mixture of Old Welsh and Latin.'

'Really? I wonder why.'

'Leave it with me for a day or two. I'll see what I can decipher. It's very worn but you've done a good job in getting what you've got on here.'

'Yes, the cat's not happy it's been cleaned up.'

'Cat? What cat?'

'It's been used as a cat's bowl for many years, I believe,' answered Gethin.

'Before you leave, where did you find it?'

'Near Offa's Dyke, on the Powys/Shropshire border.'

'Which side?' asked Huw.

'This side!'

'Good' came Huw's reply as he gently closed the door.

*

Two days later Gethin was back knocking on Professor Huw's door.

'Come in, come in!' came the shout from inside. 'Well, well! You've certainly turned up something here, young man.'

'Really! glad it was of interest and not a lame duck,' replied Gethin.

'Well, what you've turned up is an inscription that's mostly in Old Welsh, partly in Latin. This isn't a hoax, now, is it, lad?'

'No sir. The bowl is definitely real.'

'Well, as best I can decipher, the inscription says: *To commemorate the marriage of Arthur and Guinevere.*'

'No. You're joking, right?'

'That's what it says – the best I can get out of it anyway. You need to bring that bowl in for further scientific examination. What you've come across could be of great historical importance.'

Perhaps this cat bowl might prove the old boy's ramblings all along, Gethin thought. And what about the story of the sword Excalibur? Could that be lying buried in the silt out there somewhere? Now that *would* be a find!

But, he thought, did my Great Uncle Arthur ever get married? That's something I've got to look into before this goes too far.

'Don't stand there daydreaming, lad! Go get me that bowl!'

Wall Cottage

———⚬⦿⚬———

Liza Conrad was a retired civil servant; she had worked for the Inland Revenue all of her working life. Since retiring, her main hobbies had been her garden and travelling abroad. Living near the little village of Brampton, nine miles east of Carlisle in the United Kingdom, she found that the cold and wet autumn and winter weather this far north didn't agree with her ageing bones. She would take herself off to places far and wide, provided the temperatures were moderate. She loved the Greek Isles, Southern Italy, Malta ... The north coast of the Mediterranean provided many historical places where she could see out the winter months.

It was another wet and windy Monday afternoon in early February. Sat in her favourite armchair, reading her gardening magazine, she looked out on the garden and pondered a new vegetable plot. She'd always wanted to grow her own vegetables, the freshness and taste far better than what the supermarkets had to offer. Another deciding factor was the perfect specimens on offer at the supermarkets, all led by consumer demand – and at what cost to the planet?

Now, she thought, what to grow, and on how big a plot? There was no point digging a large area and then only growing a few potatoes; this whole venture needed some planning. She spied an old Percy Thrower book on her shelf and pulled it down. She thought about the vegetables she liked and what to grow and harvest in the summer months. Spending most of the winter away, it would be pointless and a waste to grow parsnips, Brussels sprouts or leeks. The thought of sprouts made her shiver anyway, the taste and texture not one she liked.

In the end she came up with a plan and hopefully over the next couple of dry days she would get to work.

She had chosen a spot that received the most sunlight in the garden and had pegged out the plot with wooden pegs and garden twine.

*

Friday morning and she was ready. With spade, fork and wheelbarrow, she started the dig. She was surprised how easy the earth surrendered to the edge of the spade, easily pushing down to eighteen inches or more without much effort. All the great gardeners of the past had advocated digging down as deep as possible to eradicate any roots but also to put much-needed air into the soil.

She was a third of the way across her plot when her spade hit something solid about twelve inches down. It wouldn't give, so she moved to dig alongside it: the same result.

Darn it, she thought, it feels big; I'm going to have to get it out. She dug a step further on, hoping to find an edge, but no such luck. Using the fork, now she estimated the size of the obstruction was approximately three metres by one and a half metres.

Establishing the centre and using the spade, she

dug down, removing the earth so that she could get a look at the obstacle.

Thinking it was an old slate slab or concrete base from long ago, the first glimpse of what she had uncovered made her step back. It looked like a decoration of some sort, a mosaic, but what was it doing in her garden?

By late afternoon, and even allowing for a break for lunch, she had uncovered most of it. She couldn't make out what the small coloured pieces were trying to tell her. She needed to uncover it all and then clean it. She could see there was a written inscription as well. Darkness came before she could complete the task, so she left it until the morning.

What could it possibly be? She knew the significance of Hadrian's Wall, and her cottage lay less than two miles to the south of it. Was there some sort of Roman villa on this spot?

She used the internet that night to trawl through as much as she could on what had been written and recorded on Roman times in her area. Nothing of any significance near her cottage came to light, so she retired to bed.

She slept lightly and restlessly. Visions of Roman legions marching up and down the wall filled her dreams.

After breakfast she was out at the excavation. A fairly large mound of earth now covered part of her once neatly mown lawn.

She dug a spade width around the mosaic; it was oval in shape. She had to be careful as she knew mosaics were easily broken. This extra dig gave her the room to undertake her next task. She filled a bucket of clean water and with an old cloth she stepped down onto the mosaic and started to clean it. The more she cleaned, the more her mouth dropped open. Once it had been fully exposed, she could see that the mosaic had been beautifully put together using very small pieces of coloured pottery and glass in very fine detail.

When finished, she stood up and stepped out of the pit and looked down at the whole thing.

The scene before her showed a crucifixion – very popular in early Roman times.

My goodness, she thought, this is a depiction of the crucifixion of Christ. The crown of thorns was clear to see, and the wound to the side. All this was shown in great detail, red blood dripping from the crown and pouring from the wound in his side.

The inscription written underneath in black and bold letters read: *Hic jacet hasta caput illius pilum.*

Well, I know nothing of Latin, she thought; I'll look into doing a translation later. What was this mosaic doing here? She could only surmise it was created by an unknown Roman person, maybe a soldier? This was a desolate spot in Roman times, and only the lowly Roman soldiers would have spent any time up here defending their realm from attack by the northern clans.

She had read somewhere that some Romans converted to Christianity, even one of the emperors, but that was much later than this, she thought, more towards the end of the Roman Empire.

That evening she sat in front of her computer and set about trying to find out about Christianity within the Roman empire, especially the soldiers. She read about Cornelius and Longinus being some of the few who converted or followed Jesus's doctrine.

What about the inscription, she thought. She typed it into Google Translate, and the answer shocked her: *Here lies the head of the spear pike.*

This can't be true, she thought. No way is the head of the spear that pierced Christ's side buried in my garden. This has got to be fake, but why do it and in such detail and complexity? She checked the internet and read that it is claimed that the original spear is held in Vienna at the Weltliches Schatzkammer museum.

Well, are they convinced they have the right one, the original? she thought. Many religious artefacts have never been proved to be authentic; many were just faked to lure in the pilgrims and, of course, bring wealth to the church.

She sat and thought for a moment. But if it is true and there is something under there, why here and why so long after – maybe up to two hundred years after the crucifixion? I'm not going to consider that option. I have my life set up as I want it now. I'm happy. Unveiling this can only bring disruption, media, onlookers, pilgrims etc. Do I want all that? No, she thought.

The next day, she photographed everything and wrote a description of its location and set about covering it over once more. When complete, she marked the centre spot and put a plan in her head that she should get something appropriate to go there – her special place where she alone could get some spiritual awareness.

She   slipped   her   written   description   and

photographs into an envelope, sealed it and placed it with her will. There, she thought. Now it will never be lost again, and in the future perhaps someone will have the courage to explore more.

Melissa

⸺❧⸺

James Howarth opened the bedroom door and peeped in.

'Hi, Peter. Everything alright? How was school today?'

'Fine, thanks.'

'Did you do much?'

'This and that.'

James gave up. Obviously Peter was involved in something special.

'Dinner ready in ten minutes, okay?'

'Yes, I'll be down now.'

'What does he get up to up there?' James asked Peter's mum Joy.

'Oh, he's always been like that, a bit secretive when he's up there, never lets on to me about anything.'

'Just seems a bit odd, what he was doing.'

'His sketches!'

'Well yes, but it looked as if he was showing them to something or someone else.'

'His special friend?' quoted Joy.

'Really, he's a bit old for that at seven, almost eight, don't you think?'

'It's always been there, ever since he was a toddler. Lying on his back, he would be giggling and drooling at something or someone at the bottom of his cot. Brightly coloured mobiles, twinkling lights, cuddly toys – nothing distracted him. He would always have eyes on the end of his cot.'

'Weren't you worried?'

'I was a single mum, trying to hold down a job. Anything to keep him amused to enable me to get on with the housework in the little spare time I had, it was a godsend.'

'Sixth sense they call it, don't they?' questioned James.

'Yes, something like that. You won't mention it to him, will you? He'll only clam up if you try.'

'I won't mention it again.'

Peter was sat cross-legged on his bed; his special friend Melissa sat opposite him, always smiling, with lovely long golden ringlets cascading down over her shoulders. Peter had always remembered her just like this. From his earliest memories, he remembered those beautiful ringlets the most. When he was tiny, she would hide her face in them and play 'Boo!' with him.

It had taken Peter months of painstaking work to establish her name. Primary school year two and three was when Peter had learnt to read and write, and an idea had formed in his head. He had never been able to communicate with Melissa, so with very rudimentary sketches at first and letters to accompany them they had together worked out her name. Melissa had never been allowed to go to school, so it was a wonderful experience for her too.

'Is dinner ready, then?' questioned Peter as he walked in the kitchen.

'Two minutes,' said Joy. 'You can help lay the table.'

'So how WAS school today?' inquired James.

'It was good, thanks.'

'How about that spelling test? How did that go?' asked Joy.

'Good, I think. I'll find out tomorrow.'

'You like English, don't you? At the last parents evening your teacher told me and your mum you were top of the class.'

'Yes, it is important to me, I needed to learn how to spell and write.'

'Does it help with your "sketch book" upstairs?'

'Oh, that. Yes, it does, a lot.'

'It's your birthday in two weeks. Is there anything specific you want or need, like videos, football boots, clothes, anything at all?' asked Joy.

'No, Mum, I'm fine for most stuff at the moment. Money to put in my savings account would be nice though.'

'We'll see what we can do,' James reassured him.

After dinner, Peter returned to his room. He didn't want to spend too much time away from Melissa. She only appeared twice a week now, and there was still lots they had to do.

Melissa was waiting patiently for him to return.

'Right!' said Peter.

Using sign language, Melissa pointed to the correct page in the scrap book. They had over the previous months concocted all the letters of the alphabet to pictures. It wasn't an easy task as Melissa had been locked up most of her life; 'd' for 'dog' didn't work, but 'd' for 'door' did.

It had been a laborious task but a few days before Peter's eighth birthday they had completed their task together.

Peter sat and read it through from start to finish, something he had been perturbed about. Reading it all now, he was shocked; he wanted to reach out and hug his friend, but he knew as soon as he tried to touch her, she would vanish. All he could do was show her he was crying, big glistening tears rolling down his cheeks. She smiled and blew him a kiss.

My name is Melissa. I was seven years old when I passed over from your world. I don't know what year it was or whether the sun was shining or was it wet and windy outside. I was kept locked in the under-stairs cupboard for most of my life, with no light or heating. The girl you see before you isn't really me. My hair is dirty and matted and itches all the time. The rags I wear are hand-me-downs from other poor children, I think.

My father started to hurt me when I was three, so my mother locked me in the cupboard to keep him away from me. I don't know which was worse, his smelly breath or the dark and cold.

In the end I just got weaker and weaker. The small bit of food my mother pushed through the door got less and less. One night I just curled up and drifted into the light ...

... although I didn't quite reach the other side. I think what stopped me was I wanted to tell my story. Not that I blame my parents in any way – I probably deserved it. I think there's a need in me to let other children who are being hurt know that there are others out there going through the same.

While lying on that dirty blanket every night I always dreamt of wearing a lovely floral-patterned

pinafore dress and my hair of golden ringlets. I'd seen
pictures of little girls like that before I was locked in.

Peter closed the scrapbook carefully and cried some more. He couldn't lift his head to look at her. When he had plucked up the courage, she was already gone. He wondered if he would ever see her again.

*

It was 8th April, Peter's birthday. He arrived home from school and rushed upstairs. Yes, she was there waiting for him. He knew then that she knew it was his birthday.

She pointed excitedly at the scrapbook and diligently spelt out a short message: *All this time and I don't even know your name. I feel different now, and I feel I can finally move on. Thank you for everything.*

She smiled one of her beautiful smiles and waved as Peter spelt out his name.

He saw her lips moving. He was sure she said *Peter.*

Slowly her shape shrank to a small bright light. The light gently rose above the bed and after traversing the room at high level, with a small flash it disappeared. Peter sat there for a few minutes, not moving, not even thinking. He felt emotionally drained, as if the light he had just witnessed had taken part of his life with it.

He closed the scrapbook, gave it a big hug, then pushed it under his bed and lay back, big tears rolling down the sides of his face.

Invasion

— ❦ —

Nic Richardson partner in RCA Architects was at his office desk 7:30 pm on a Monday evening in late June. His office window was open, letting in a refreshing cool breeze. He had recently returned from a five-day visit to Nigeria. He rubbed the back of his neck as he studied his initial draft of elevational drawings.

This was a commission the firm had received to design a new building to house 20th-century African art. Nic had taken a short break from work and decided to kill two birds with one stone and take a well-earned holiday break. He had chosen Lagos in Nigeria where he felt there was a good mix of old and new buildings, a bustling port and culturally very African. He had hoped a mix of this and different cultures would provide him with the inspiration he needed. Lagos also had good-quality hotels for him to relax in for a few days. Nic was forty and single with no family ties or pets, giving him the freedom to work and travel as and when he wished.

He rubbed the back of his neck again – annoyingly, an insect sting on his second day while walking around the port. This unfortunately had resulted in a large lump forming, but this had receded after twenty-four hours, so he hadn't bothered with medical advice. He had put it down to a mosquito and left it at that. Since returning, though, he had suffered with nausea and a bloated feeling in his abdomen, which was a bit troubling.

While he worked tweaking a roof line here or a base line there, he felt his shirt tighten around his abdomen. Feeling a little uncomfortable he unbuttoned the shirt; he watched his abdomen grow larger and larger. The pain was increasing immensely as his skin stretched and his internal organs collapsed. Suddenly, emerging from his belly button, there was a thin black tendril.

This tendril, as it protruded more and more, lashed about as if trying to get purchase on something.

Nic stood and now in excruciating pain he tried to stagger back but the tendril had latched onto the leg of his desk, and with enormous strength it pulled him down again. Nic screamed, well he wasn't sure whether any sound emitted the pain was excruciating and enveloped his whole being.

The creature inside him, now it had managed to grab onto something solid, pulled harder and harder until it burst out of Nick's abdomen, leaving a gaping hole ten centimetres across. As the creature left, its last act was to use one of its thin, pincered legs to stab into Nic's weakening heart. Nic was dead in seconds.

The creature, completely black in colour, stood approximately 50 centimetres tall, on six thin but strong legs. The tendril it had used to extract itself from its host had detached itself and was writhing around on the desk under the creature's legs, like another being.

The creature was just a black blob, with six long legs. It had smooth skin and no discernible orifices. It

115

stood there, its body moving up and down as if panting, or maybe pumping life into its six limbs.

A minute later it scurried across the desk, down to the floor, up the opposite wall across the ceiling and lowered itself down into one of the ceiling up-lighters.

Heather Jones was office manager at RCA Architects and was always early, arriving before anyone else. She liked to have a good tidy around before the rest of the staff arrived. She went to unlock the door and was surprised to find it already open, and that's when she saw Nic sat in his chair facing away from her. His demeanour looked odd; she imagined him fast asleep, and she called his name while crossing the room. Nic didn't stir, so Heather walked up to his side, and on seeing the blood and gore she let out a terrible scream.

As the office door opened the creature rose out of its refuge, crawled across the ceiling, down the wall to the door frame and left. It had made its way across the corridor ceiling and reached the bulkhead of the stair-case as the caretaker of the building rushed up the stairs.

Jim Faraday had been caretaker at Ashley House, where RCA Architects had their second-floor office, for two years. He had never heard a scream like it. He made it up the stairs in double quick time. Finding the horrific scene, he grabbed an office phone and dialled 999.

Heather was sobbing uncontrollably. Jim put his arm around her and helped her up from her kneeling position. After sitting her down in her chair well away from the carnage, he walked over to Nic and with slow, calm fingers he eased Nic's eyelids down over his cold, staring eyes.

He walked back to Heather.

'I'll stop anyone else coming up. Are you alright here for a while, or do you want to come with me?'

'No, I'll stay here with poor Nic for now. The police won't be long' she sobbed.

Jim made his way back to the foyer. At the very top of the stairs, head down, he suddenly felt a slight stinging sensation on the back of his neck. He rubbed it vigorously as he made his way down the two flights.

Jim knew all the RCA staff by name, and he held them all now in his small office. He explained there had been a tragedy upstairs and that all would be explained later.

Creature No. 1, from its vantage point on the ceiling above the staircase, had felt the presence of a new host below. Carefully and deliberately, it had ejected a tiny dart from its right front leg. Each leg had a dart, and the creature's aim was to unleash them all in the short time it had left. The creature's time was limited by the fact that its only sustenance was within itself. The process was to find enough human hosts, six preferably, to continue the creature's life cycle. Traversing the panelled ceiling of the long corridor, the creature found a loose tile. Lifting it up it carefully squeezed into the gap above and waited.

9:30 Tuesday morning after Jim's night shift he was in his kitchen making himself a bacon sandwich when Ingrid his wife walked in.

'Oh God, what's that lump on the back of your neck?' she asked.

Jim rubbed the spot without thinking.

'Oh, nothing, just a bite. I think it'll go; it's not

hurting, if that's what's worrying you. If it's still there tomorrow, I'll make an appointment to see a doctor.'

'Do that. It doesn't look natural!'

The following Friday evening and Jim was sitting in his favourite armchair watching the early evening news. Every third weekend a private security firm would take overlooking after Ashley House, giving Jim a well-earned break to spend time with his family. Ingrid was making them both dinner in the kitchen.

Jim had felt uncomfortable all week, a niggling pain in his stomach and a bloated feeling in his abdomen. He put it all down to stress and anxiety following the discovery of Nic's body.

It was 6:30pm and Jim was catching up on the regional news stories. He was hoping that something would be revealed about Nic's demise, but nothing was mentioned.

Suddenly he felt pressure in his abdomen. His torso was enlarging, putting pressure on his usually loose-fitting tee shirt.

He pulled up his tee shirt; it relieved some of the pressure, but it was still building inside.

Suddenly he watched with horror as a small black tendril emerged through his belly button. The pain in his abdomen became almost unbearable as his skin stretched and his internal organs were squeezed. The tendril extended and whipped around, looking for purchase. When it finally gripped onto a draw knob on a nearby cabinet it pulled with one mighty jerk and the creature ejected out of Jim's torso, killing him as it left.

As Ingrid walked into the lounge, she was halfway into telling Jim the TV was on too loud when she dropped the tray she was carrying and screamed.

Mavis Jarvis in the flat below jumped with a start as the tray hit the floor above.

'Right, I've had enough. I'm going to give those two up there a piece of my mind'.

She stormed up the flight of stairs and knocked on the door to No. 17. No one answered so she tried the handle, and the door opened just wide enough to reveal the horror inside.

The creature, now free of its host and the tendril, had found a space between two books on a bookshelf. Creature No. 2 had menacing dark eyes. It had been resting there while pumping up and down, but now, seeing the door open, the creature took its chance. It left its hiding place and, using the room furniture as cover, it swiftly left the flat. Silently it crossed the corridor floor and headed over to the staircase. It squeezed through the balustrades and traversed the ceiling below, down the wall over to the next set of balustrades. Three flights later and it was in the main foyer. It crept across the smooth plastered ceiling. It found a place above a timber cupboard housing the service meters, where it rested, watched and waited.

*

Jake Summers, a community paramedic first responder, had taken the call from central control at 6:40 pm. He got on his 500cc Kawasaki GPZ and sped around to Winton Heights – a block of flats he knew well. Jake's day job was a firefighter, but on his days off he volunteered as a first responder.

He reached the block in less than two minutes. Racing through the foyer and up the stairs, he didn't see the creature – but the creature saw him.

Jake checked Jim's vitals and declared him deceased at 6:45pm. A doctor or senior paramedic was needed to officially confirm this, but Jake knew his assessment would be accepted by either.

Police officers and ambulance staff arrived quickly, and Jake found himself with nothing more to do, so he slowly made his way down to the ground floor.

The creature was aware and felt him coming. Jake made it to the foyer, head bowed, still traumatised by the vision up in Flat 17.

The creature took its opportunity and carefully struck with a dart from its left front leg.

Jake felt an instant sharp pain on the back of his neck, nothing more. He slapped his hand on his neck to feel for something, a natural reaction.

He felt nothing so carried on out into the night.

*

Next morning when Jake woke, Steve, his partner, was already up and in the kitchen, making breakfast.

'Busy night, was it?' Steve asked as Jake walked in.

'Yes, rather. A troubling case. I can't discuss it, you know that, don't you?'

'Yes, I do, and I don't think it's fair you have to burden yourself with it all.'

'Patient confidentiality.'

'Call it what you like, talking about it would help. Wait – what's that lump on your neck?'

'Oh, I don't know, it's nothing, I'm sure.'

'Well, you should know, but I don't like the look of it!'

Jake was on shift at the fire station for the next four nights. He arrived back at his three bed semi he shared with Steve at 8:15 am.

Steve was already up and in the kitchen, making coffee and crumpets.

'Take a seat. You look a bit peaky.'

'Ah it's nothing, really. Just feeling a bit bloated, that's all.'

'I'll make a peppermint tea, that should help,' Steve reassured him.

Jake sat down, but the pain was slowly overwhelming him. He ripped off his shirt, hoping that would help, but all it did was reveal a black tendril emerging from his abdomen.

Steve screamed first.

'My God! What is that!' was all he could muster.

'Cut it off, for goodness sake, cut it—'

Those were the last words from Jake.

The tendril had lashed itself around the table leg and with one quick movement it had extracted itself from Jake's now limp body.

Steve, now with a blade in his right hand, moved towards the creature. The tendril, although now detached from its jet-black host, flew upwards and wrapped itself around Steve's arm.

Steve screamed again, dropped the blade and tried to lash at the thing wrapped around his arm with a blunt knife he'd lifted from the kitchen table.

All this time, Creature No. 3 was waiting patiently, pumping extra life into its six long legs. Its piercing eyes scanned the room, but more worryingly this creature had a mouth with serrated teeth and was now salivating at the thought of sustenance.

Creature No. 3 was now ready to feed. Steve's eyes bulged as the creature moved deliberately towards his face.

CPSIA information can be obtained
at www.ICGtesting.com
Printed in the USA
LVHW110835170919
631332LV00001B/80/P